SLOW HEAT

With stories by

Celeste Anwar
Alicia Sparks
Kimberly Zant

Erotic Contemporary Romance

New Concepts   Georgia

Be sure to check out our website for the very best in fiction at fantastic prices!

When you visit our webpage, you can:
* Read excerpts of currently available books
* View cover art of upcoming books and current releases
* Find out more about the talented artists who capture the magic of the writer's imagination on the covers
* Order books from our backlist
* Find out the latest NCP and author news--including any upcoming book signings by your favorite NCP author
* Read author bios and reviews of our books
* Get NCP submission guidelines
* And so much more!

We offer a 20% discount on all new Trade Paperback releases ordered from our website!

Be sure to visit our webpage to find the best deals in e-books and paperbacks! To find out about our new releases as soon as they are available, please be sure to sign up for our newsletter (http://www.newconceptspublishing.com/newsletter.htm) or join our reader group (http://groups.yahoo.com/group/new_concepts_pub/join)!

The newsletter is available by double opt in only and our customer information is *never* shared!

Visit our webpage at:
www.newconceptspublishing.com

Slow Heat is an original publication of NCP. This work has never before appeared in book form. This work is a novel. Any similarity to actual persons or events is purely coincidental.

New Concepts Publishing, Inc.
5202 Humphreys Rd.
Lake Park, GA 31636

ISBN 1-58608-825-4
© 2006 Celeste Anwar
© 2006 Alicia Sparks
© 2006 Kimberly Zant
Cover art (c) copyright 2006 Eliza Black

All rights reserved, which includes the right to reproduce this book or portions thereof in any form whatsoever except as provided by the U.S. Copyright Law.

If you purchased this book without a cover you should be aware this book is stolen property.

NCP books are available at special quantity discounts for bulk purchases for sales promotions, premiums, fund raising, or educational use. For details, write, email, or phone New Concepts Publishing, Inc., 5202 Humphreys Rd., Lake Park, GA 31636; Ph. 229-257-0367, Fax 229-219-1097; orders@newconceptspublishing.com.

First NCP Trade Paperback Printing: October 2006

Table of Contents

Cajun Heat — Page 5

Underneath It All — Page 57

Blood Feud — Page 123

Cajun Heat

By

Celeste Anwar

Chapter One

Yveline Tebeau flattened herself against the ground, not because she feared being spotted at the moment, but because every muscle in her body was protesting the awkward position she'd been holding for what seemed like hours. The moment she did, she was certain she could feel crawling things inching under her clothing.

She had not realized just how much she detested the woods until she'd decided to pursue the story that had just seemed to drop into her lap like manna from heaven. She had tried everything else she knew to try to land a job as a real journalist, but one look at her seemed to be all it took to convince people she wasn't serious.

She didn't know what the hell it was about her looks that made them think that, but she was sure when she presented them with the gritty story she was in pursuit of that all that would change.

The cabin she'd been staking out for almost a week was reputedly a rendezvous point for a sex slave ring. *That* was news, real news, hard and gritty and shocking. It was going to be a serious wakeup call once she broke the story.

If she got the story.

Resisting the urge to check her clothes, again, for ticks or any other crawling thing, she picked up her binoculars again and focused them on the cabin after a brief search for the image in the lens that made her dizzy.

There wasn't a sign of the man she'd seen there the past two days.

No sign of a car for that matter, but she was no idiot. He could have left the car in a hiding spot and hoofed it to the cabin.

She'd been there a while herself though, and she hadn't seen the 'sex god' coming or going--that was the mental tag she'd given him because the guy was be-u-ti-ful to behold, all kinds of nice, rock hard muscle and swarthy skin, black, black hair. He was sooo dangerous looking he made her kegels flutter every time she caught a glimpse of his black brows and narrowed, predatory eyes. Made her think of a pirate or something.

Hours had passed since she'd crawled to her vantage point for a look. One anyway, and there'd been no movement at all in the cabin.

He wouldn't be asleep at this time of the morning.

A thrill of both excitement and fear surged through her the moment her mind suggested that this might be the opportunity she'd been hoping for.

Actually, she'd hoped the gang would show up with a group of captives so she could get pictures. But that hadn't happened and she was getting tired of playing guerilla, crawling along the ground on her hands and knees, or her belly, peering through binoculars, ducking for cover whenever she heard any sound at all that she couldn't identify.

Which had been pretty much everything when she'd first arrived, because she wasn't used to being in the woods and *nothing* was familiar.

Sighing, certain she did feel something wiggling up her belly, Yveline dropped the binoculars and pushed herself up to her hands and knees and then sat back on her heels to examine the crawling sensation.

It was a millipede. She had to resist the urge to scream the moment she saw the thing. Flicking at it with her fingers, she shuddered all over when she'd managed to dislodge it.

That cinched it. She wasn't going to lie in the woods while wildlife fed off her if she didn't have to. There was a good chance she would find something in that cabin to substantiate the rumor she'd heard. Now was the time to check, while nobody was around.

She was too uneasy to just march right up to the front door, she discovered. She'd darted behind three different saplings before it dawned on her that she probably wasn't hidden if anyone was watching. She was no stick. She preferred to think of herself as pleasantly plump, or voluptuous, but she knew in this day and time when beauty was measured in ounces, most people just thought she was fat--or volumptuous.

She had a trim waist, she thought defensively, but wide hips and big boobs translated to fat when the clothes never touched her waist.

Pushing her insecurity to the back of her mind, even though it was her volume that had prompted the thoughts to begin with because she wasn't actually built for speed, she looked around for a little bit broader tree trunk before she made the next daring dash.

She was a nervous wreck by the time she'd reached the cabin, mostly from scaring herself. There hadn't been any sign that anyone was about, not a sound out of place except her thrashing progress through the dead leaves and brush that littered the forest floor.

Pausing to catch her breath and try to get her heart under control before she passed out from excitement, she glanced around one last time and darted toward the porch.

The door wasn't locked.

Trying to convince herself that that wasn't because there was nothing inside to find, but rather because the cabin was so deep in the woods, and so well hidden, that they hadn't thought it necessary to lock it, she depressed the latch and pushed the door slowly open, peering through the widening crack.

There was only one room, thankfully.

When she neither heard nor saw anything, she pushed the door wider and darted inside.

The door slammed behind her. Two hands grabbed her in a hard grip and shoved her back against the wall. A hard body plastered itself on top of her, sandwiching her between board and board hard abs.

Yveline didn't know if there was any pain involved in the move or not. The shock of suddenly being seized when she'd thought she was completely alone threw her instantly into a state of catatonia. Discovering that she was gaping at a face full of pecs, she tipped her head back slowly to look up at the monster that had grabbed her.

It was the dark, dangerous looking sex god she had been drooling over through her binoculars for days. She felt her jaw sag to half mast.

"What are you doin' here? Who sent you?"

His voice was sexy, too. The husky drawl with just a trace of Cajun accent cut right through her like a hot knife through butter. Caught between sheer terror and total enchantment to discover he looked even better close up, Yveline's mind didn't catch one word out of five.

Gritting his teeth when her only response was to gape at him mindlessly, he grabbed the neck of her blouse, giving it a jerk that popped every button off. That caught her attention, dragging her gaze from the sex god.

She stared down in dismay at the utilitarian 'harness' she had to wear to keep her boobs from beating her to death. No skimpy, sexy, lacy confections to support these monsters! It took the bra equivalent of a forklift. Her skin looked like paper next to the dark hands that stroked along her belly, and then her back, and finally grabbed her bra straps, jerking them down her arms so that her breasts spilled out.

He stared down at her bobbing, jiggling breasts for several moments as if he'd completely forgotten where he was. "No wire," he said a little hoarsely.

Yveline licked her dry lips, trying to force her mind to function. It finally dawned on her that he'd thought she was a cop, but that only made her more uneasy.

If he'd slam a cop against the wall and strip her, he wasn't going to be intimidated about her being a reporter--sort of.

In fact, that might make him more hostile.

Because it had finally penetrated her stupor that his expression was grim and she was pretty sure that was bad news.

"I was … uh … was … supposed to meet a guy here," she stammered out finally, hoping she could convince him it was just a mistake that she'd stumbled into the cabin. "At least … you know … I think I might have the wrong cabin."

His dark, demonically arched brows snapped together over the bridge of the 'noble' nose she'd been rhapsodizing about. His lovely mouth, which she'd coveted in her dreams, tightened.

She could see he was reassessing the situation and he wasn't happy about what was going through his mind.

"Take your clothes off," he growled after a prolonged moment in which Yveline had time to consider whether it had actually been a good idea to approach the cabin after all. He snatched her shoulder bag off and stepped away from her.

Yveline swallowed audibly, blinked. "What?"

He gave her a look through narrowed eyes that promised lethal retribution if she questioned his authority again. "Take dem off before I take dem off for you."

Enlightenment blindsided her.

He thought she was a slave, one of the many women duped by some ruse or other into putting themselves into the hands of the sex slave traders. The lie she'd thought up to cover herself had fit perfectly with the typical scenario.

She would've felt brilliant except for the small matter that she'd actually intended to make an *excuse* for her appearance. She hadn't been trying to convince him she was supposed to be there.

Headlines flashed in her mind's eye--*Lousiana woman found dead in the bayous.*

She blinked and a fresh headline flashed into her mind, this time with her byline. *An insider's look at the sex slave trade.*

Adrenaline shot through her that was two parts sheer terror, one part excitement, and one part--arousal--because she was *insane*! And she'd been lying in the woods for days fantasizing about the gorgeous hunk that was currently threatening her life.

She could see he meant business.

A shiver of anticipation went through her in spite of every attempt to will sanity back into her brain.

She decided not to complain about the fact that he was rifling through her personal belongings.

Grasping the snap on her pants, she unfastened them. When she'd nudged her sneakers off of her feet, she hooked her thumbs in her pants and pulled them down to her knees.

"The panties and bra, too."

She stared at him, wishing she'd trimmed her hedge into one of those cute, sexy little heart shapes or something like that.

And worn a thong instead of the granny panties and granny bra she was wearing.

God!

In the presence of a sex god and she wasn't even wearing sexy lingerie! Damn it to hell!

Reflecting that she at least probably looked the part of an 'innocent'--they always grabbed the inexperienced women because they were perfect victims--she reached behind her back and unfastened the bra and then slipped her panties down her legs and stepped out of the panties and the jeans she'd been wearing.

Tossing her bag across the cabin, he snatched her clothes out of her hands and examined them, checking the pockets.

He pulled a leaf and a beatle out of one and Yveline flinched, wondering if he'd figure out from that, and the dirt ground into the jeans from the knees up, that she'd been crawling around on the ground. She hoped not because she didn't care for that first headline. The second one, the one she was going to write *after* she'd experienced being a sex slave first hand, was much more to her taste.

* * * *

Jake Duvall stared down at the clothing in his hands, hardly aware of what he was looking at as he struggled with his dilemma. He'd *had* to do something about the woman he'd seen watching the cabin for the past several days, especially since she'd decided to come into the cabin to investigate. As long as she'd stayed outside, he figured he could pretend he hadn't noticed her.

That would've been bad enough. They'd think he wasn't worth a shit as a lookout, but now he was going to be in real shit if he let her go and it turned out that they'd sent her to keep an eye on him, maybe to test him.

He knew he hadn't been accepted yet or they wouldn't have stuck him down here in the damned cabin in the middle of the styx. They would've given him a real assignment--like moving some product, which would've given him the chance to look for the girl he'd come for.

But as irritating and nerve wracking and just plain boring as it had been hanging around with nothing to do but wait, he'd still felt like he was making some headway in his assignment, and he'd actually been relieved to be bored instead of neck deep in something illegal as hell, besides being completely unpalatable.

He'd known going into this that he might have to do some things he would rather not, just to convince them he wasn't a cop, but he hadn't expected what he was facing now. He'd thought he could avoid, somehow, actually abusing any of the women--which was how the men controlled them.

She must be a test, he decided, feeling a little sick. They must have arranged the meeting to see what he'd do, to see if he had the balls to work for them.

A cop wouldn't touch the girl, and they'd think, right away, that he was a cop if he didn't. He wasn't, but they weren't going to give a fuck that he was a private investigator and it wouldn't make much difference to him, either. He was going to be just as dead.

The problem was he wasn't sure he had it in him to rough the girl up.

He knew damned well he couldn't if she kept looking at him with those bambi eyes of hers. Maybe, if she screamed at him and fought him, but not when she looked so soft and innocent and fragile.

He hadn't been sure he could even get a hard on until he'd seen the size of the melons that fell out of her bra. That had had an instant and very positive effect. But could he maintain it if he had to make her have sex with him, that was the question?

He wouldn't have minded seducing her. Hell, under other circumstances that would've been just what he was doing, because there was no getting around the fact that she was as fine a piece he'd seen in a while. But if she was a plant, it sure as hell wasn't going to make him convincing to sweet talk his way into her pants.

And that was what he *had* to do if he wanted to live long enough to get the girl he'd come for and get out of the gang again with his hide intact.

He wondered if the money the girl's father was paying him was going to comfort him when he was in jail for raping bambi.

If she'd just kept her nosy ass out in the woods, he wouldn't be facing this fucking dilemma! "What's your name?" he growled angrily.

"Yveline," she said in a husky gasp that sent currents of arousal through him.

"Well, Yveline--this is how it works. You do whatever I say, whenever I tell you t'do something, and you get ta live."

She gave him the bambi look again.

He grabbed her hair. "Do you understand?" he growled, leaning down to glare at her almost nose to nose.

She nodded jerkily.

"You're one of the boss's girl's now, but obviously they sent you here to me for your initiation so what you're gonna do is suck me off." He thought that over for a moment. "An' if you bite me, I'm gonna to loosen your teeth."

Her wide eyed gaze moved from his face to his crotch.

He caught her chin in his hand. "I don't wanna hurt you. Don't make me."

Her gaze flickered over his face. It made him uncomfortable on two levels.

First and foremost, he had the gut churning feeling that she was memorizing every feature and was going to be able to repeat it in great detail when and if she managed to get to the cops.

Secondly, she looked so vulnerable and innocent he felt sick to his stomach and wondered if she even had a fucking clue of what 'suck me off' meant.

She couldn't be that innocent, he told himself. She looked like she must be in her twenties anyway. She *had* to have had some sexual experience.

They'd just picked her because she *looked* so young and innocent.

"Get down on your knees."

She sank to her knees so promptly he thought it was at least partially because they'd given out with fright. Gritting his teeth, trying not to think too much about it, he unfastened his belt and dragged it from the belt loops and then unfastened his jeans and pulled his cock out.

She gave it that bambi look and his cock instantly sprang to attention.

After glancing up at him anxiously a couple of times, she lifted a hand and grasped it. The pleasure that went through him as he felt her hand close around him almost made him black out.

All doubts about whether or not he could do it, fled. Mesmerized, he watched her soft, full lips part, watched as she took the head of his cock into her mouth, wondering if he was going to lose it the moment he felt her tongue curl around his shaft.

* * * *

Yveline felt her throat go dry as she heard the man command her to perform oral sex on him. As scared silly as she was, she could not shake the feeling that she'd just entered 'fantasy sex world' and been handed a sex god to play with.

She had *never* gotten this close to a man that looked as good as he did in her life before. Actually, she'd never gotten close to one that looked half as good.

She'd only had two boyfriends in her life and both of them had been 'nice,' not handsome, not exciting-- nice. Which she'd appreciated, of course, but she'd found the sexual side of their relationships tepid, to say the least.

His cock was as impressive as the rest of him. She couldn't imagine why a guy that looked as good as he did would even want to take part in a sex slave ring, but she supposed the money was good, and maybe he got off on being masterful and demanding.

She had never thought she would get off on being submissive, but everything on her body was tingling and fluttering with excitement and anticipation and she hadn't even touched him yet.

Dragging in a shaky breath, she reached to catch the golden dong nervously, more than half expecting him to slap her hand and tell her she couldn't have it after all. When he didn't, she leaned toward him and covered the head with her mouth, tasting him experimentally.

Pleasure wafted through her. He tasted as dreamy as he looked. Shuffling a little closer, she began to stroke him with her hand as she guided his cock into her mouth slowly and out again, stroking the length of his shaft with her mouth and tongue.

She'd known it would come in handy to watch all of those sex therapy shows!

A shudder went through him. Her body reacted with heat, and excitement, and a growing tautness to his response to her and she began to suck him with more and more enthusiasm as the pleasurable tension curled more and more tightly inside of her.

He caught a fistful of her hair, clenching his fingers tightly. A hoarse groan escaped him. Tremors began to run through his body. He braced a hand against the wall behind her as if he could no longer maintain his balance without the support.

The muscles along her passage constricted as she felt his rising desire, heard the sounds he couldn't contain that told her how much pleasure she was giving him. Moisture gathered inside of her sex. Her heart began to labor so that she felt dizzy from the rush of blood through her body, ached from the need climbing higher and higher inside of her.

His hands kneaded her shoulders, clamped against her head, and then returned to her shoulders, as if he hardly knew what he was doing. His breathing became ragged, punctuated by short, breathless grunts.

Abruptly, his cock bucked in her mouth.

This was where she usually retreated.

He'd said suck him off, though.

Feeling a fiery rush of power and pleasure, she worked her hands and mouth over his cock more feverishly, sucking him, stroking his balls. He uttered a choked groan as his seed spilled into her mouth. She swallowed, sucking him harder, until he was shaking all over, gasping hoarsely, until she'd sucked him dry. His hands fisted in her hair.

She heard him grinding his teeth as he pushed her away.

She yielded reluctantly, gasping for breath, her body still ravaged with need.

He stared down at her for a long moment, his eyes glazed, and finally moved across the room and sprawled weakly in a chair. Running a shaking hand over his face, he jerked his head toward the narrow cot along one wall. "Get in da bed."

Rising shakily, Yveline did as she was told, hoping he meant to master her some more because her body was screaming for release.

The cot, to her relief, looked and smelled as if the sheet had been changed fairly recently. Settling on the edge, she tried to decide whether she was supposed to lie down or not. Finally, she lay down, curling onto her side because she just wasn't comfortable lying on her back with the weight of her breasts compressing her lungs and she was so aroused she was having enough trouble getting a decent a breath as it was.

His gaze had followed her as she moved to the bed. When she lay down on her side, he scanned her thoroughly from her breasts to her hips and the curling thatch of hair that covered her mound. Pushing himself out of the chair abruptly, as if he'd come to a decision, he pulled his shirt off and tossed it aside, pushed his shoes from his feet and then crossed the cabin, staring down at her as he shoved his jeans and shorts off.

His cock was hard again, as stiffly erect as if she hadn't just thoroughly sated the man. Anticipation went through her when she saw his gaze on her breasts.

"On your back," he murmured.

When she rolled over, he grasped the leg nearest him and pulled her thighs wide, settling between them and then leaning over her.

She jumped at the electrifying jolt that went through her when his mouth covered the tip of one breast, closing her eyes tightly at the intensity of the sensation. The fire that had not been appeased, that had scarcely even died down a fraction from performing oral sex on him, surged upward to envelope her. Within moments, she was panting for breath, her mind a whirl with the intoxicating sensations pounding through her as he teased the painfully swollen tip with his mouth and tongue until she thought she would come.

She dragged in a shaky breath when he lifted his head at last, but the relief was short lived. Grazing her skin with his lips, he crossed the valley to the other peak and tortured it with his mouth and tongue as he had the first until she was nearly mindless with the fire burning through her, desperate to find release and almost equally frantic to hold out a little longer, to wait until she could feel him plowing into her.

Stroking a hand down over her belly, he explored her cleft with his fingers, caressing her clit and sending another hard jolt of pleasure through her that nearly sent her over the edge.

She fought it, desperate to hang on until she felt his cock inside of her.

As if he'd read her mind, he ceased teasing her with his finger and grasped his cock, guiding it along her cleft until he connected with the mouth of her sex. She bit her lip as she felt him probing her.

When she opened her eyes, she saw that he was watching her face as he pressed into her. His expression was harsh with need, his eyes dark with it. She spread her thighs wider, lifting to counter his thrust, gasping when she felt him slip deeper, felt the stroke of his hard flesh along the walls of her channel.

He lifted slightly away from her, looking down to watch as their bodies slowly merged. Letting out a harsh breath abruptly, he burrowed his face against the side of her neck and thrust hard, burying himself to the hilt with a bruising pressure that felt so good she wanted to scream. She bit her lip, straining toward him.

Shifting his hands beneath her buttocks, he dug his fingers into her flesh as he withdrew and drove into her again, withdrawing slowly and driving into her over and over, increasing the pace a little faster each time until he was pounding into her like a pile driver, grindingly. Her heart pounded with the excitement coursing through her veins. Her cunt tightened with each driving thrust, grasping at his thick cock like she could hold onto him and keep from slipping over the edge.

The force of his thrusts inched her up the bed despite his hold on her. It drove her over the edge into neverland, too, made her come so hard and suddenly she uttered hoarse cries of ecstasy as wave upon hard wave of rapture exploded inside of her in sharp convulsions that drained every ounce of strength from her body and left her as limp as a wet rag and weak as water.

She shuddered all over, gasping for air, every muscle twitching with unequivocal pleasure.

Her cries or her paroxysms of pleasure, or both, sent him over the edge. Releasing a harsh breath, he began to shudder, driving into her frantically and finally collapsing weakly on top of her when he'd emptied his cock of semen deep inside her.

Neither of them moved for many minutes. Drifting in blissful contentment, Yveline struggled to make a few mental notes on her first foray into the life of a sex slave, wondering a little dazedly if she was going to be able to remember the 'notes' when she finally managed to commit them to paper.

Chapter Two

More thoroughly sated than he could ever remember being in his entire life, Jake wanted nothing so much as to drop into oblivion the moment his body stopped convulsing in release and left him completely drained. He knew he was probably crushing the breath out of her, however. Gathering himself with an effort, he levered himself off of her after a while and climbed off the bed since it was too damned narrow for both of them to lie on it. Propping his ass on the edge of the bed for a moment, he leaned down to retrieve his jeans and shorts from the floor and finally straightened and moved the chair again, too tired even to consider putting them back on at the moment. Sprawling in the chair naked, he dropped the wad of clothing in his lap and sat forward, his head in his hands, trying to decide if all the screaming and thrashing she'd been doing was from the throes of passion or because he'd pounded into her hard enough to buckle her spine.

A shudder went through him at the memory and he felt his cock stir.

Mentally berating the insatiable beast, he slid a glance at the girl--woman. She looked young, but she wasn't built like a girl. She was all woman--all soft tits and ass and tight pussy.

He wanted her again and he hadn't even recovered from the last bout.

"Could I ... go to the bathroom?"

He lifted his head at the sound of her voice, studying her for several moments while he tried to decide if she was asking because she thought it might give her an opportunity to escape, or because she wanted to wash him off of her, or just because she needed to relieve herself.

She looked scared, but he couldn't see anything to indicate that she was skating the edge of hysteria. Jerking his head in the direction of the door finally, he watched her through narrowed eyes as she got up and went into the bathroom.

There weren't any windows. He didn't need to watch her. He supposed he should, because he was supposed to be breaking her spirit, but he was pretty sure if he went to watch her he was going to want to fuck her again. And he wasn't convinced his heart could handle another climax like the two he'd just had until it had had a little down time.

So much for thinking he might have a problem performing because of the circumstances.

He had the uncomfortable feeling that at least a part of his overactive libido had to do with the circumstances, though, that he was turned on at least partly because he could tell her to do whatever he wanted and she did it. If she'd fought him, or screamed, or behaved as if he was torturing her, things might have gone differently.

He was reasonably certain they would have in spite of the fact that he found her so desirable.

She'd been aroused, though, as aroused as he was. He was sure he hadn't imagined it. She'd sucked his cock--not just until she'd sucked him dry, but until he'd thought he was going to pass out.

That was enthusiasm above and beyond the call.

Unless, of course, she hadn't completely understood the 'suck me dry' part and/or was too scared to know when to stop.

He knew damned well he hadn't imagined the groans and soft cries had been from pleasure, though. He'd felt her body convulse with release. That was what had sent him over the edge, the way her pussy had caught a stranglehold on his cock, milking him.

He grew hard again thinking about it.

He studied her through narrowed, hungry eyes as she came out of the bathroom. She had an arm across her breasts, but her arm didn't begin to cover the half of them and he could see one pert, pink nipple poking between her fingers.

Instantly forgetting that he'd decided he needed to rest before he could even consider going another round, he got up and strode toward her when she stood outside the door uncertainly. It occurred to him that she was probably trying to gather the nerve to ask him if she could get dressed. He probably ought to let her, too, before he hurt himself, but he was too caught up in the game now.

Everything about her--from the fragile, hopelessly lost expression on her face, to her abundant to curves, to her submissive manner had set his libido into overdrive and he had no desire to tame it until he'd thoroughly and completely sated himself on the woman.

Or dropped dead in the attempt.

Catching her arm, he led her to the bed again, and made her sit on the mattress. Settling at the other end, he pushed her onto her back and told her to draw her knees up and spread her legs. She stared at him wide eyed for a moment, but complied before he had to tell her again. After studying the nest of light hair at the apex of her thighs, he pushed them wide, his gaze focused on her pussy. Finally, he reached down to part the flesh and study the bright pink inner lips, stroking the thin, sensitive pedals of flesh and feeling blood begin to pound harder and harder in his cock. It was beautiful. His mouth went dry with the need to taste it.

Lifting his head, he studied her a moment. "Get up."

Looking surprised, she did. When he'd settled himself more comfortably on the bed on his back, he grasped his cock and told her he wanted her to suck him off again. She got down on her knees. "Up here. On all fours."

Frowning, she studied his position on the bed and finally climbed up as he'd told her, facing the opposite direction. A jolt when through her when he spread her legs wide and rubbed his fingers along her cleft as she covered the head of his cock with her mouth and began stroking him. Catching hold of her thighs, he dragged her to him until he could fasten his mouth over her clit, sucking her as she sucked on him, on fire the moment he tasted her delicate flesh. She moaned, caressing him with more enthusiasm as he alternately teased her clit with his tongue and sucked at the tiny nub.

The pleasure was mind blowing. As badly as he wanted to hold off and enjoy it longer, he felt his body skyrocketing toward explosion. He felt her come that time on his tongue, felt the tremors, felt it in the feverish movements of her mouth and tongue on his cock that brought him to orgasm within moments of her peak.

She didn't stop until his body was thoroughly drained.

Nearly unconsciousness, it occurred to him that he was either in heaven, or in love--or *he* was the one rapidly becoming a sex slave. As exhausted as he was, he was torn between the desire to seek oblivion and an equally compelling desire to turn around on the bed and shove his cock into her pussy and keep driving into her until he couldn't move anymore.

Dimly, he realized he had a new problem. He'd fucked himself into exhaustion and he was going to be really fucked if she waited until he passed out and sneaked out on him.

He'd probably wake up with a half dozen cops standing over him.

Dragging himself up with an effort, he looked around a little dazedly for something to tie her up with and finally made her get up so that he could use the sheet.

After tearing it into strips, he made her lie down again and tied her spread eagle on the bed.

It was probably not one of his better ideas, because it just made him want to fuck her again, but fortunately his cock failed to rise to the occasion. Crawling over her, he cupped one breast in his hand and used her other breast as a pillow and yielded to his exhaustion.

* * * *

By the time the man tied her up, Yveline had reached a point of exhaustion that precluded fear. She hadn't even realized she'd been wound up and tense until he'd worked all that nasty old tension right out of her till she'd felt doughy and malleable all over. And just plain exhausted.

In the back of her mind, even while she'd been enjoying herself hugely, she'd known she was in a ticklish situation. She'd realized she was a prisoner-- sex slave. That was part of what she'd found so titillating about the whole business.

Actually, she supposed it was more like icing on the cake.

The guy was gorgeous enough just to look at to make her cream in her jeans. The possibility of actually being with him had never entered her mind, and then there was the danger factor that shouldn't have made him appealing at all but did. Tied up together in a neat little package that included an insatiable lust for her, she'd been so swept up in her fantasy she hadn't adequately considered her situation until he'd thoroughly exhausted her and then tied her up.

And then gone to sleep.

She'd even been in to the bondage thing while he was tying her up and she'd thought he was doing it to fuck her some more.

He hadn't though, and it was borne in upon her that it wasn't a bondage thing. It was imprisonment.

She still liked the new story idea she'd come up with. As gritty as the story was that she'd planned to do, it paled beside the actual experience.

She just wasn't sure any longer that she wanted to do the story from an insider's perspective, not when it had finally dawned upon her that it meant she was going to have to screw a *lot* of men--men she hadn't picked.

It went without saying that it was very unlikely they were going to be hunks like this guy. Maybe some of them wouldn't be bad looking, but they were probably pigs or they wouldn't have to pay for sex.

Or they liked really weird shit that women didn't want to do.

She would've been perfectly content to be *his* sex slave for a while, but she knew it didn't work that way. He'd inducted her. Someone would come to pick her up and install her in a whore house somewhere. Or he would take her to them.

Mentally, she chided herself for being a total wimp. There was nothing 'gritty' about what she'd been doing. The guy hadn't even slapped her once. She doubted she would have a single bruise to show for her 'harrowing experience' as a sex slave.

And obviously, he was nothing but a look out--not even actually a member of the gang yet, if she considered what he'd said about being tested.

Which meant he also probably didn't know much more, if any, than she did about the ring. She wasn't going to be able to pump him for information.

She might get pumped some more, and she thought she'd probably enjoy it, but it wasn't going to get that story written for her.

It didn't take a lot of tugging at the bindings to figure out that, as tired as he'd seemed when he'd done it, he had still managed to fashion some really tough knots. They weren't tight enough to cut off her circulation, but she couldn't pull her hands out of the loops and tied spread eagle she couldn't reach any of the knots with her teeth.

Lifting her head, she surveyed the cabin for anything that might look like damning evidence. She couldn't exactly see all that well splayed out on the bed with the guy lying half on top of her, but it was easy enough to see there wasn't a lot in the cabin period.

In fact, aside from the cot and the chair he'd been sitting in, she only saw a refrigerator and a sink and a few shelves, mostly empty.

It wasn't a place where they stayed. It was just a rendezvous point.

They probably brought at least some of the women in through the swamps.

She was staring up at the ceiling trying to figure out how she was going to get herself out of the mess she'd gotten in to when the guy roused. Still more than half asleep, he began to nuzzle the breast he'd been laying on. Warmth spread through her immediately. It was heightened in short order by his tongue, which he thrust from his mouth and flicked at her nipple with until it was standing erect and pulsing with the rapid beat of her heart. When he'd teased it until it began to ache with sensitivity, he sucked it into his mouth.

The effect was like a shower of fireworks, hot sparks stinging her from shoulder to groin and moisture pooling in her sex in invitation. Yveline closed her eyes.

Cooperation was one thing, but she'd realized it probably wasn't a great idea to convince the guy that she relished her situation, if for no other reason than the fact that he would be trying to convince the boss that she was ready to ship.

Her best chance of escaping was going to be *before* they caged her in one of those places where they wore the women's spirits down until they didn't dare object to anything they were told to do.

Closing her eyes didn't help. The fire crept insidiously along her nerve endings as he continued to tug at her 'antenna.' Closing her eyes just meant focusing on that keenly sensitive receptor.

Opening her eyes didn't help either, not when she looked down, watching his face, watching his mouth as he worked on her nipple with true dedication. Within a few moments her sex was clenching and unclenching as if calling him to dinner.

He moved over her, lifting away from her just enough to ram his cock into the mouth of her sex while he caught her other nipple and tortured it a while. Grunting in satisfaction when he made the connection, he settled, pumping almost lazily until he'd managed to gain complete possession of her passage.

Unable to help herself, she tipped her hips up each time he thrust inside of her, whimpering when the bindings prevented her from feeling him as deeply as she needed.

He seemed to realize the limitations about the same time she did.

Pulling away, he untied her ankles. Instead of merely pushing her knees up, though, he caught her calves and lifted her legs straight up. On his knees now, he probed until he connected again and then watched his cock slip into her and out again, stroking her so slowly she thought she was going to lose her mind, or pass out from holding her breath, waiting in painful anticipation for the next thrust, or retreat that would caress her cunt the way she needed it.

She couldn't arch to meet him, either, with her legs in that position, couldn't get any leverage to force him to move faster, drive deeper. All she could do was gasp and hold her breath and gasp in another sharp breath.

He paused after he'd tormented her until she was ready to scream at him. His dark gaze met hers for a pregnant moment. Releasing his grip on her calves, he allowed her legs to rest against his shoulders and he bent toward her. The movement lifted her hips free of the bed, pushed her legs wider. That time, when he thrust, she felt him hit bottom. She sucked in a sharp breath as waves of intense sensation went through her.

Leaning lower still, he set a faster pace, driving into her so deeply he was grinding his belly against her cleft and then withdrawing almost completely, then thrusting deeply again.

The turmoil inside of her grew chaotic.

"More?"

Yveline swallowed at the question, fighting the urge to beg for more.

He withdrew, pulling all the way out.

She bit her lip. "Yes. More."

A tremor went through him.

"More, Jake," he murmured.

Her gaze flew to his face. Dimly, she realized he was demanding that she acknowledge that she wanted it as much as he did, that she was giving. He wasn't just taking. It piqued her, but he had to know she was willing. She hadn't tried to pretend otherwise. "Jake, I want …. I need it."

Satisfaction and desire hardened his features. He shoved his cock head into her again, drove deeply.

She gasped as she felt his shaft stroke her g-spot all the way down, making her quake inside, making her hunger for more. "More," she demanded as he began to withdraw.

He thrust again, but she could see he'd begun to tremble with the effort to hold his needs at bay to tease her. She uttered a faint moan as he sank into her again, lifting to meet him.

Groaning, he stilled for a moment and then abruptly shoved her legs aside and burrowed against her. Wrapping his arms tightly around her he set a rhythm that was as desperate as his first claiming, driving into her in hard, deep thrusts that were almost as painful as they were pleasurable, stroking the deep itch that desperately needed his touch.

She was gasping so hard and fast when her body exploded with ecstasy, she thought for several moments that she would pass out. Blackness, fire and light exploded in her body and in her mind with a concussion that was so hard she was surprised she didn't fly apart.

She was barely conscious when she felt him shudder with his own release.

It was the strain on her arms that finally penetrated the haze that enveloped her afterwards. She shifted, trying to get comfortable.

He lifted his head with an effort, stared at her face blankly for a moment before his gaze traveled up her arms to her wrists. Frowning, he shifted upward and untied them. She winced when the circulation began to return in a stinging tide.

Grabbing her arms, he rubbed them and finally rolled off of her. "Get up."

She was wobbly legged when she had managed to struggle off the bed. Grasping her arm, he led her into the bathroom.

The bathroom was tiny, the shower more like a coffin than a shower. Adjusting the water, he shoved her in and followed her. They had to stand practically chest to chest, but that didn't seem to bother him. He bathed her, focusing mostly on her breasts and her pussy.

She supposed since he'd thoroughly explored both, that was what needed bathing most, but it was a lot more stimulating than it should have been.

"What did you do before, Yvie?" he murmured huskily as he held her against the shower wall and pushed his fingers up inside of her.

He mind was already clouded with the stimuli, but her sense of self preservation wasn't totally lost to her. "I just graduated," she finally managed.

He frowned. "College?"

That sent a jolt through her, because she realized he thought she was younger than she was. Was *that* why nobody took her seriously when she was trying to get a damned job?

She considered for several moments before she answered. "Yes," she finally said.

He seemed relieved.

That seemed strange to her. Wouldn't he have been happier if she'd been younger, she wondered? They liked them young.

"What was your degree in?"

That seemed like a stranger question than the first. The guy had her pinned to the wall of the shower and four inches of finger buried in her pussy. She doubted it was in the nature of 'getting to know' her. For that matter, she didn't see why he'd care on a business level. The slave traders weren't interested in the women's minds.

Unless he'd begun to suspect she hadn't just fallen into a trap?

She remembered her fucking camera then. "Photography--wildlife photography," she added for good measure.

He moved closer, pushing her legs apart and replacing his fingers with his cock as he closed his mouth over her ear. Shivers traveled over her as she felt the heat of his mouth, the teasing exploration of his tongue. Leaving off after a moment, he hooked a hand under her chin and pushed her face up. "Baby, I had no idea I was going to enjoy my job this much," he murmured, covering her lips and stroking them with his tongue until she opened for him.

They came together that time. The water was cold by the time they staggered out weakly and dried off.

There was only one towel, and Yveline was still damp when they emerged from the bathroom. Weak, she didn't even ask. The moment he released his grip on her she headed for the cot and collapsed on it face down.

Jake stared down at her rounded buttocks, resisting the urge to join her. After a few moments, he went to collect his clothing and pulled his shorts on. Deciding he didn't currently have enough energy to put the jeans on, he sprawled in the chair, tipping his head back against the padded back and staring at the ceiling.

Working her out of his system wasn't working, he realized wryly. The more he plowed her furrows, the more possessive he felt about her.

Or maybe obsessive was the more accurate term.

He frowned at that thought as it occurred to him for the first time to wonder why they'd sent him a woman that looked like Yveline to test him. Unless the 'test' had been to see if he could keep his hands off the merchandise, which he'd failed grandly, it seemed a little odd that they would have sent him such a tempting morsel of female flesh.

Of course, they only picked the pretty, vulnerable type anyway. Nobody wanted to pay for ugly, even if all they wanted to do was poke her in the ass and never saw her face, and the fighters were hard to break without killing them he supposed, or fucking them up so badly that they were useless.

He got up after a moment, pulled his pants on and strode across the room to pick up her bag again. He hadn't paid it much attention the first time he'd looked through her stuff. His mind had been totally focused on those magnificent breasts of hers.

There was a digital camera in the bottom. Pulling it out, he looked it over and saw that it had a preview screen. Moving back to the chair with the bag and the camera, he found the button and began to flip through images.

All of them were of the cabin. Most of them had him standing at the window, or in the door, or coming out, or going in.

Fuck!

A cold sweat broke from his pores. He shoved the camera back into her bag and began to check the contents of the bag again, finally dumping everything out on the floor.

There was a tiny voice recorder, too.

God fucking damn it!

She was either an investigator, like he was, or she was a damned reporter!

And he'd just spent the last several hours fucking the hell out her like there was no tomorrow!

Shoving everything back into her bag abruptly, except for the digital camera and the recorder, he threw the bag across the cabin angrily and shoved her recording devices into his pants pockets.

Now what the hell was he going to do?

He glared at her when she turned her head to look at him, but he discovered he couldn't sustain his anger. She gave him that wide-eyed doe look again that turned his belly, and his brain, to mush.

As exhausted as he was from fucking her already, he wanted to march across the room right then and fuck her a few more times. Hell, he might as well! He couldn't be any more screwed than he already was!

Grabbing up the stuff he'd dumped on the floor, he shoved it back into her bag angrily and finally got up. Striding across the room, he grabbed her clothes, wadded them into a ball and threw them at her. "Put them on!" he growled.

He had to get her out of the cabin before anybody showed up. He knew with gut churning certainty now that she was *not* a test, she was not one of the captives--unless he counted the fact that he'd taken her captive.

There was going to be hell to pay in letting her go--for him--because she'd be able to recognize him and she was probably going to haul ass for the nearest police station, but that couldn't be helped now. He wasn't going to compound the trouble he was already in by turning her over to the boss or any of his lieutenants.

He'd been trying to infiltrate the ring to find a girl and free her. It had been no part of his plan to help them grab anybody else, particularly in light of the fact that it had already been bothering the hell out of him to think of giving Yvie up to them.

He ran completely out of luck before she'd managed to do more than drag her bra and panties on.

He heard a car pull up outside. Striding to the window, he peered out just as the guy he knew as 'Jinx' got out of his SUV.

"Fuck!" he snarled, turning to glare at Yveline. "We're both fucked now! I hope to hell that dumb blond look of yours is deceptive, because if you don't do *exactly* what I tell you to, and go along with me, we're both in deep shit."

Chapter Three

Indignation swelled in Yveline's breast at the suggestion that she was a 'dumb blond.' She happened to have graduated at the top of her class, damn it! Before she could inform him that her looks were certainly deceptive if he had gotten the idea she was just some bimbo, a hairy beast slammed the cabin door open and lumbered into the room.

Jake was dark and dangerous looking in a sexy way.

This man was just plain scary. Black curling hair sprouted from every inch of exposed skin, including his ears, and the back and shoulders revealed by the sleeveless, 'wife beater' undershirt he was wearing.

Everywhere, except the top of his head.

He had the Ben Franklin look going on for him. The hair that *was* attached to his skull was long and stringy and greasy looking. His wild kingdom eyebrows drew down in a furious scowl when he spied her.

Her mouth dried up with sheer terror. Her entire body dried up.

"What's with the girl? You fucking stupid, or what? She your girlfriend?"

Jake's face was a mask, but she could see he was debating whether to claim her or not. Apparently, he decided that wasn't the best route. He shrugged easily. "I happened to see her and figured the boss would like her looks."

The beast grunted.

"She's too fat. Boss don't like the fat ones."

Yveline sucked in an outraged gasp, her gaze flying to Jake.

Jake looked thoroughly pissed. "Are you fuckin' blind, or what, Jinx? She's built like a brick shit house," he snarled. "Fine! If you think the boss won' want her, we'll just drop her in the middle of the swamp and let her find her way home--if she can. She's beautiful, but not terribly bright. I didn' realize that at first. I think she might be a little retarded, if you know what I mean. She didn' give me a bit of trouble."

The beast he'd called Jinx glared at him, but Yveline could see that Jinx wasn't terribly bright himself. "Cain't let her go. She's been in the cabin. She's seen both of us."

Yveline felt her stomach drop to her toes.

Jake looked a little pale himself. "Why don't we just let the boss decide if he wants her or not? She's a hell of a fuck. And, like I said, docile. I didn't have to slap her around much and she was perfectly willing to do anything I told her to do. Come here, baby, and show him those beautiful tits of yours."

Yveline reddened. She didn't want to get near the brute, but she knew the moment she saw 'Jinx' that Jake had been right about them both being in deep shit. Swallowing her reluctance with an effort, she moved to Jake obediently and allowed him to pull her bra off.

Jerking her around until her back was to him, he pulled her against his chest, cupping a breast in each hand and displaying them.

Jinx stared at her breasts much the same way Jake had, except that it made her stomach churn.

"Why don't you have a seat while I put her through her paces?" Jake suggested when Jinx lifted his hand like a sleepwalker as if he would grab her breast.

Nodding, Jinx flopped down in the chair Jake had just vacated.

It took all Yveline could do to keep from glaring at him, but she saw it would've been a wasted effort anyway, when she looked up at him. His face was closed, hard. "Take off the panties, bitch, and get down on your knees."

Shaking, she did as he told her. "You're going to have to get me ready," he ground out.

Blinking as he shoved his jeans and shorts down, Yveline saw he was having performance anxiety himself. His cock was flaccid.

On the other hand, they'd been fucking for hours.

There was something about the look in Jake's eyes that told her she was going to be performing with Jinx if she didn't get a rise out of him, though. Dragging in a deep breath, she grasped his cock and began to lick and suck at him, stroking his flesh. To her relief, his cock responded at once, growing hard.

She thought he was relieved, too. Pulling her to her feet after a few minutes, he led her to the bed by one arm and made her lean down with her ass in the air. She couldn't figure out why until she realized she was facing the wall. She wouldn't have to look at Jinx.

He wouldn't be able to see much of what was going on, either.

Apparently Jinx realized that, too. He got up and moved the chair to a better viewing angle as Jake shoved his fingers into her and began to stroke her. Her body responded immediately to his touch, in spite of the situation, growing moist. The heated languor stole over her.

Removing his fingers, he replaced them with his cock and began to thrust into her.

She grabbed two fistfuls of mattress covering to keep him from shoving her head into the wall, bracing herself as he quickly increased his pace to a pounding thrust.

She supposed she shouldn't have found it stimulating. The thought of being watched should have dried up her desire. It didn't. She didn't know whether it added to the heat building inside of her, but it sure as hell didn't prevent it.

She didn't try to hold back. They were performing for their lives and she went with the flow, moaning with rising excitement as she felt the delicious stroke of his cock along the walls of her pussy. Her breasts swayed with every thrust, brushing back and forth across the rough fabric of the mattress and sending heat surging through her as if they were being caressed.

Almost on the thought, he leaned over her, cupping one in each hand, pinching them and sending harder jolts of pleasure through her. Her body quaked, trembled on the verge of release and then the tension shattered, dragging a hoarse cry from her as bliss thundered through her.

He came almost on top of her culmination, distress in his hoarse groan as his body bucked and ejaculated his seed into her.

For a moment, he settled heavily against her but apparently he felt the tremors of weakness running through her. He pushed himself upright with an effort, letting out a hiss as he pulled his cock from her.

Weakly, Yveline crawled onto the bed and collapsed.

She heard the chair squawk along the floor as Jinx shoved himself out of it. "You're right. Looks like a nice piece of ass. I'm going to have a go at it."

Yveline tensed all over.

Jake's voice was almost casual, but she thought she detected anger threading it. "Guess the boss wasn't in any particular hurry then?"

Jinx stopped. "Huh?"

"You weren't sent to pick me up?"

"Fuck! I forgot all about it!"

Still he hesitated, obviously reluctant to give up on the idea of getting some before he left. "I'll ask the boss when we get there," he said finally. "We're supposed to move some girls today. Bring the girl and hurry it up. We're running late."

Relief flooded Yveline, but more than just relief. She was going to get to see the gang, and the girls, and the place where they would be handling the rendezvous!

"Get dressed, Yveline," Jake growled. "You heard him. We're movin'."

Still shaky from her release and about as scared as she was excited at the prospect of getting her story, Yveline rushed to comply, trying to ignore the sticky residue between her thighs although she would've far preferred to get the chance to clean up.

The musky scent of sex still clung to her and she didn't like the way Jinx kept looking at her and licking his lips.

She didn't actually want him looking at her at all.

Jake gripped her arm when she'd tied her shirt together--he'd popped all the buttons off and it was the best she could do.

Unfortunately, it didn't cover her that well. Jinx had snatched her bra from her before she could put it back on and tossed it over his shoulder.

Frowning, Jake tightened his hand on her arm and led her from the cabin, pushing her into the back of the SUV and then climbing into the front. "Behave yourself," he said as she settled into the seat.

She supposed that was a warning not to try anything.

She was tempted to anyway as Jinx got into the driver's seat and headed out. She wanted the story, badly, but she'd no sooner settled in the backseat of the vehicle than she began to wonder how she was going to get herself out of the stable once they'd put her in it. There weren't many that managed to get out on their own. That was one of the things that made their enterprise so successful. They could do anything they wanted to with the women, use them as long as they wanted to, and then dispose of them when they decided the girl wasn't useful anymore.

She didn't want or need to get that deeply undercover to get the story.

Furthermore, she realized that the main reason she hadn't been scared absolutely shitless from the very beginning was Jake. Once she passed from his hands, there was no telling what they would do with her.

She was staking a lot on him anyway.

God! He might not be 'in' with them, but he was trying to get in.

Maybe he was right and she was an idiot, a well educated moron, but still a fool.

There was no opportunity to try to escape though, even after she'd finally tumbled to the fact that she needed to. Short of trying to open the back and dive out, she was trapped, and she was pretty sure she couldn't get the back open and leap from the thing before Jinx managed to stop the vehicle.

And she was positive she couldn't outrun Jake and Jinx both, probably neither one of them. No way could her short fat legs compete with their long lean ones!

And then Jinx would probably beat the ever loving hell out of her and she wouldn't be in any condition to try anything else.

She didn't think Jake would.

She didn't *know* he wouldn't, but she didn't think he would.

They left the woods after about thirty minutes. The way she'd approached it had taken her at least forty five, so she wasn't sure of where they were going at first. They did return to the city, contrary to what she'd begun to think. They just circled around and approached from a different direction.

After thinking it over, she decided Jinx must have taken the round about route to make sure they weren't being followed.

She wasn't sure. He kept looking in the rear view mirror, but his gaze seemed to linger on her--or more specifically her boobs, which were bouncing around like two fighting puppies.

She was going to be sore from all the jiggling, but she supposed she would be getting off lightly if that was all.

She'd had a half formed thought of leaping out of the SUV when they finally let her out and screaming bloody murder for help. The area of the city where Jinx took her, however, wasn't an area that cops generally liked to ramble around in--especially at night and the sun had already set by the time they reached the run down warehouse. A few street lights had winked on, but for the most part the lights were either broken or they just didn't work.

Along the way they passed several houses that were readily identifiable as crack houses. Refuse littered the streets. Derelicts sprawled along the broken sidewalks, leaning against the falling down buildings behind them, or pushed buggies filled with all sorts of junk. Prostitutes stood on the street corners and titty bars alternated with package stores along the block before they reached the warehouse.

Screaming, Yveline reflected, probably wouldn't be noticed. She had a bad feeling that that particular sound was heard pretty frequently in the area.

By the time Jinx pulled the SUV over, she was scared totally shitless and she'd forgotten all about the glorious headlines she was going to grab with her 'gritty' story.

Jake helped her out. "Just keep your eyes on me, baby," he muttered, leaning toward her and whispering the words against her ear. "If I say run, run like hell and don' look back."

Hope surged through her at that, and another wave of weakness that made her knees feel like putty.

He meant to try to help her!

He was outnumbered and the others had guns she saw as soon as they reached the door, which was barred by a guy that looked far more dangerous than Jinx, mostly because there was intelligence and suspicion in his eyes as he surveyed Jake and Yveline. "What's with the piece of ass? Nobody told me you'd be bringing a bitch."

Jinx grinned from ear to ear. "I found her! Look at her tits!"

The guy looked them over. It was obvious from the way he glanced at Jinx that he was impressed.

Yveline repressed the urge to sigh irritably. God! Give the guys balls to play with and they were like delighted children!

She wasn't going to object. She'd spent most of her life hating the fact that very few people ever looked above her bust line. Even women tended to look them over speculatively, and critically, as if they were weighing the possibility that the boobs were fake.

They were real! And she had the bad back to prove it, by damn!

She was going to get a fucking reduction just as soon as she made enough money.

She'd never considered they might be a life saver, though, except maybe to act like built in life preservers if she ever fell overboard--which wasn't likely since she hated boats.

It transpired that they were the ticket inside, though, with few questions asked.

Jake's hand tightened on her arm as they moved through the door and into the poorly lit interior of the warehouse. Inside, the place looked almost worse than it had outside. There was litter everywhere, and the strong scent of urine suggested that more than mice inhabited it.

Crates were stacked sporadically along what Yveline supposed had once been aisles where forklifts had moved up and down to shift the crates around. As they moved deeper into the warehouse, their progress marked by the sound of their feet echoing eerily around the place, the stacks of crates gave way to stacks of metal containers of the sort pulled by semis.

Near the back end of the warehouse, three dark SUVs and a paneled van had been parked. About a dozen men were scattered around the vehicles, all of them armed with automatics and scanning the warehouse suspiciously.

A man dressed in a business suit got out of the backseat of one of the SUVs as they came into view. Yveline felt like her heart was going to break free of her chest as she saw him.

She knew this must be the boss.

He looked like a pimp on closer inspection. The suit was definitely high dollar, but his black hair was slicked back on his head and tied in a ponytail at the base of his skull and she could see a tattoo along the side of his neck.

Probably an old gang tattoo, she deduced. Most of the big crime people had started out in a small way as young thugs.

His accent was thick when he spoke, but she couldn't quite place it, only that it wasn't an accent she was familiar with.

"This the new man?"

Jinx nodded. "This is Jake Duvall, boss."

His gaze barely grazed Jake. "Who's the woman?"

"I found her, boss. Figured you can make some good money off this one."

'Boss' slugged Jinx so hard, so swiftly, that Yveline didn't even have time to gape at him. Jinx rocked backwards and slammed into the hood of the SUV, denting it. "Do I pay you to think?" he asked coldly.

Wiping the blood from his lip, Jinx stared at the man with a mixture of fear and anger. "No."

"Why don't I pay you to think?"

"Because I'm stupid?"

Moving past Jinx, he stopped when he was toe to toe with Yveline, catching her jaw and tilting her face up to inspect it. "Where did you find her?"

Yveline felt weakness filter through her, at the man's touch, the coldness of his eyes, but mostly because Jinx was a moron. He'd lied about finding her, and she didn't think he had the brain power to back the lie up. Jinx shrugged when the boss turned around to look at him. "She was broke down side of the road. There wasn't anybody around."

"You're sure about that?"

Jinx nodded vigorously. "I looked real good."

"If you've led the cops to us, you're going to be gator bait," the boss growled. He'd turned his attention to Yveline again, however. She flinched when he very calmly untied her blouse and examined her breasts. "Nice," he commented, squeezing them experimentally. "You didn't do badly at all, Jinx. You've got a good eye."

He caught her chin again. "Are you a trouble maker?"

Yveline's eyes widened. She tried to gather moisture in her mouth to speak, tried to gather her wits to think of something to say.

Apparently, her silence was the best thing she could've done, though.

"She's dumb," Jinx offered. "Alls I had to do was slap around a couple of times and she was willing to do anything I told her to do."

Ok, so Jinx was a few cards shy of a whole deck, but he was good at repeating whatever he'd been told.

The boss 'patted' her cheek, hard enough it rattled her eyeballs in her head. "Put her in the van and let's get the others out."

Jake surged forward to grab her arm. "Not you. You can help us unload the others."

Jake didn't look at her as Jinx caught her arm and led her to the back of the van. One of the men that had been checking out the warehouse moved to a container and unlocked it. Jake joined him, helping to open the doors. When the doors were standing wide, Yveline caught a glimpse of a wad of women huddled in the back corner. Jake leapt up onto the deck of the container and strode purposefully toward the women in the back. "On your feet!"

Whimpering, uttering frightened sounds like small animals, the women scrambled to their feet and began to scurry toward the back of the container.

Jinx shoved her into the van before she got the chance to see more, but she discovered once she was inside, that she could see the unloading through the front windshield of the van.

Jake, she saw, had followed the women out. He had one hand firmly clamped on the arm of a blond girl that didn't look to be much more than thirteen--fourteen at the outside. Her breasts were virtually non-existent, but then she was skinny as a rail anyway. Leaping down, Jake reached up again for the girl and swung her down behind him.

The procession of men and battered women was nearing the van where Yveline was when complete chaos erupted. Flood lights pinned everyone so that they froze. "FBI! Lay down your weapons and freeze!"

The command to drop the guns and freeze had the opposite effect. The men and women had already frozen beneath the glare of the floodlights, but the voice command over the bullhorn unfroze them. Abruptly, they scattered in every direction, the men spraying short bursts of bullets at everything that could conceivably hide a Fed.

Screaming, half the women flattened themselves against the concrete floor and the rest ran either ran around in circles or darted away in search of cover.

A bullet hit the windshield. It exploded into flying chunks of glass.

The door of the van was wrenched open. "Yvie! Come on!"

Yveline's heart leapt up into her throat. Without even considering whether it was a good idea or not, she scrambled toward him. He still had a grip on the little girl, she saw. Grabbing her arm with his other hand, he glanced around quickly and dragged them with him to the nearest stack of containers.

Gasping for breath, he halted, grabbing the girl's face. "Becca?"

Her chin wobbled. "Nobody calls me that but daddy."

"Your father sent me to bring you home. We've gotta get out of here first though."

Ushering them along on either side of him, he raced down the length of the row of containers and stopped at the other end. After glancing around quickly, he grabbed them and headed toward the back of the warehouse, where they'd entered. About half way down the wall, they saw an opening where someone had broken into the warehouse and cut the metal siding, bending it back.

Jake dropped down on his knees and peered out, then motioned for them to precede him. Becca scrambled out first, and then Yveline and finally Jake.

They found themselves in a narrow alley. From the sound of the sirens, cops were converging on the area from every direction. Grabbing each of them by an arm, Jake herded them down the narrow alley and then turned down an alley that ran perpendicular to it.

When they'd covered nearly a city block, he drew them to a stop.

"Becca's father was clear on what he wanted--no cops, no questioning her, no court. I have to agree with him. The kid's been through enough. And, I might add, I've got no desire to spend the rest of the night trying to explain why we were in that warehouse, so, unless you'd rather go t'the cops than come with me, Yvie, here's the plan. We stroll down the sidewalk bold as brass--you two are going to play hookers, and, if we make it through the check points, we're home free. If they stop us and ask questions, let me do the talking."

Yveline exchanged a look with Becca. Becca didn't look like she was in any condition to handle an investigation, poor kid. She was bruised and battered and Yveline seriously doubted they could get past the cops without drawing attention, whatever Jake thought. She didn't have a better plan to suggest, though. "I'm game if Becca is," she said finally.

She didn't need the interrogation to do her report, and she wasn't any more anxious to try to convince the cops that she wasn't involved than Jake was. She didn't have anything to prove she was a reporter-- because she wasn't, not officially. They might just figure her for a victim, but they might decide she was part of the pick up.

Becca nodded.

Draping an arm over Yveline's shoulder and wrapping one around Becca's waist, Jake herded them down the alley as if they had all the time in the world. Yveline glanced at him several times, because as they progressed, he seemed--almost drunk--but she finally decided that he'd added the drunken weave for effect. They encountered some suspicious glances from the cops they passed, but apparently the cops were more interested in the group they'd rounded up in the warehouse. After a few probing questions, they were allowed to pass.

Jake managed to hail a cab several blocks down the road, and they piled in.

Shaky with relief, Yveline drooped against the seat.

"Where to?" the cabby asked.

Jake glanced at Yveline and then gave the guy the name of a hotel.

It wasn't until they'd paid the driver off, that Yveline discovered that Jake was bleeding.

She'd wondered why he seemed to lean more heavily on her the longer they walked. "Oh my god! You're shot!"

He shook his head tiredly. "Grazed. Hurts like a son-of-bitch though."

Fishing into his jeans pocket as they reached his room, he pulled his key out and unlocked the door, ushering them inside.

It was a pretty run down hotel but reasonably clean.

As soon as they were inside, Yveline helped Jake to the bed and began tugging at his shirt. It was stuck to him, which she took as a good sign meaning the blood was clotting already, even though he let out a yelp when she pulled it loose and glared at her.

Relieved when she saw he hadn't minimized the situation, she went into the bathroom for washcloths when he flopped backwards on the bed. "Call your father," he murmured a little dizzily, turning his head to look at the girl. "The number where he's stayin' is by the phone."

When Yveline made it back into the room, the girl was cradling the phone, sobbing.

Jake hissed when Yveline placed the hot bath cloth against the raw track along his ribs.

"Sorry," she murmured. "I don't think this is going to need stitches but you should probably get them to look at it at a hospital anyway. I imagine they'll want to give you a shot."

"Thanks, but I don' think so. They'll see it's gunshot wound," he muttered. "Anyway, I need t'get the girl to her father."

He met her gaze. "Are you all right?"

Yveline shuddered. She hadn't really had time to consider whether she was all right or not. The whole experience had just been too much to take in. "I don't honestly know. I guess I'll know when the shock wears off."

He looked at her uncomfortably. "About what happened at the cabin...."

She shook her head, glancing at the girl. "I don't actually want to talk about that right now either," she said shakily. "I'm going home."

He frowned, but he didn't make any attempt to stop her as she moved to the door. She paused when she'd opened the door. "Bye Jake."

Chapter Four

Yveline managed to make it all the way back to her apartment and lock herself inside before reaction set in. She'd been holding it at bay with a strenuous effort for what seemed like an eternity. The moment she locked her door behind her, however, and felt secure for the first time since she'd left her apartment, everything that had happened closed in around her.

Cold, shaking with fear, she headed to her bathroom, stripped off her clothes and took a long, long, hot bath. Nothing had really seemed real to her until Jinx had arrived at the cabin in the woods. She'd been unnerved--all right, Jake had scared the pee out of her at first, but she hadn't been deep down scared until reality had smacked her in the face upon Jinx's arrival.

Maybe, she thought, she really wasn't cut out to be a journalist?

Maybe all those people that had given her the brush off were right and she had no business trying to do real news?

She lay awake most of the night, checking the news to see what was being reported about the bust of the sex slave ring. It was all over the news, but apparently the cops and the FBI were being pretty closed mouth about it because no one seemed to know for certain just what had been going on in the warehouse.

In the wee hours, she finally managed to shake off her fright enough to sit down and begin the story she'd risked her life to get.

It didn't turn out quite the way she'd planned it. She found herself glossing over her initiation into the stable of sex slaves, and focusing on her impressions of the big boss, and the rescue of a frightened little girl by a stranger.

She supposed the FBI were the real heroes, and she should have given them credit, but she didn't feel like giving them credit. Jake had risked his life infiltrating the group to find the girl.

No doubt he'd been paid well to do it, but it wasn't like the FBI and the cops actually risked their necks for nothing either. They got a pay check, too.

Anyway, it was patently obvious the bust had been well coordinated. That meant the victims had suffered god only knew what while they were 'organizing' and they'd been right in the middle of the gunfight.

Jake deserved the credit. He'd risked his life to save *her* too, and risked jail time, and he hadn't been paid for that.

She didn't name him.

She supposed she would've felt entirely different about the whole thing if she hadn't welcomed his creative way of handling the situation. The fact was, though, that the time she'd spent with him was the only bright spot in the whole debacle.

And she missed him.

She supposed she wouldn't see him again, but he was a hell of a lover and she wouldn't have minded, at all, getting to know him a *lot* better--a lot longer.

She had to wait for hours to talk to the 'guy in charge' at the newspaper, but finally she was allowed into his hallowed presence.

"I was at the bust of the sex ring last night," she announced without preamble.

"So were half the reporters in town," he said dryly. "And the TV crews."

She stood up and put her story on his desk. "I was inside before the cops and the FBI got there, and well before any of the news reporters. I was there when they unloaded the women from the back of a semi trailer. I almost got to be one of their stable of girls, because I've been staking out this story for weeks."

He glanced at her sharply at that. Grabbing the print out off his desk top, he scanned through it quickly.

When he lowered it, he looked her over with more interest. "Not bad."

Her lips tightened. "It's better than not bad."

He shrugged. His gaze flickered of her assessingly. "You look more like a front desk girl."

It wasn't a compliment. "So maybe it's an asset *not* looking like a serious reporter?"

He didn't exactly agree with her, but he didn't exactly disagree either.

He *did* give her a job.

The paper *did* run the story.

Two weeks later Yveline was neck deep in digging up dirt on a local congressman when someone knocked at her door. Surprised, she lifted her head, waiting for another knock to be sure it was actually someone at her door and not one of the other apartments.

When the knock came again, she got up from the floor where she'd been working and hobbled to the door.

Jake leaned against the door jamb when she opened the door, her purse swinging from his finger by the shoulder strap--the purse she'd left in the cabin when she'd been hustled out to meet the big boss.

She took it, wondering if that was the only reason he'd come--it explained how he'd found her, but not why he had come to look for her.

He studied her for several moments. "You gonna invite me in or scream the house down, Yvie?"

Yveline felt warmth flood through her. "That depends on what you came to do," she said finally.

His dark brows shot upward in surprise. Amusement and heat gleamed in his eyes. Shoving away from the door, he stalked her as she began to back into the apartment. Giving the door a push as he stepped inside, he looked her over from head to toe. "Take your clothes off and I'll show you."

Her hands shook as she unbuttoned her blouse slowly, dragging the hem from her jeans. When she unbuttoned it to the bottom, she allowed the shirt to slip from her shoulders and float to the floor.

Unfastening her jeans, she pushed them down her hips and then leaned down to pull them off her legs.

His gaze slid over the matching thong and bra she was wearing. She'd felt sexy when she'd gotten them, special order over the net--sexy, lacy underwear, bra size double d--and she felt even more sexy when she saw the look in his eyes. "The bra and panties, too," he said, his voice husky.

Reaching behind her back, she unfastened the bra and allowed the straps to slide down her arms, dropping it to the floor before she hooked her thumbs into her thong and removed it.

He pulled his shirt off, moving closer.

"Now, this is how it works. You do whatever I tell you to do, whenever I tell you to do it, and … if you're a good girl, I'll fuck you till you scream."

She stared at him wide eyed for a moment and finally nodded slowly.

"Get down on your knees. You're going to suck my cock until I come."

Yveline licked her lips, allowing her gaze to slide down his broad chest to the bulge in his jeans. Slowly, she dropped to her knees, waiting, watching him as he unfastened his jeans and pushed them down his hips. His cock, rock hard and glossy with the blood engorging it, sprang free.

Her mouth watered. Her pussy wept. Lifting a hand, she grasped his turgid flesh and guided it to her mouth. He tasted sublime. She'd almost forgotten how much he excited her, thrilled her. Hunger arose inside of her.

His hands closed on her shoulders as she stroked and sucked his flesh feverishly, feeding her own desire as she drove him closer and closer to completion. Tremors began to move through him. Uttering a harsh groan, he moved his hands from her shoulders to her head. His fingers tightened on her skull for several moments.

"God, Yvie! Your mouth feels so damned good."

A rush went through her, excitement and anticipation colliding inside of her dizzyingly. Moving closer to him, she grabbed his buttocks, moving faster as she felt the faint tremors escalate to hard trembles.

He uttered a choked sound, caught his breath and groaned as his cock bucked in her mouth, trying to pull away. She tightened her grip on his buttocks, took his cock as deeply into her mouth as she could and sucked hard. His fingers dug into her shoulders, he swayed, groaned as his body abruptly yielded up his seed.

She pulled on his flesh, sucking him hungrily until his knees abruptly gave out and he jerked free of her grasp.

He leaned against her, gasping harshly to catch his breath. Finally, he caught her face between his palms nuzzling her face with his, nipping at her lips.

"Lay down," he said gustily, releasing her after a moment.

She glanced around.

He looked at the litter of papers, as well. "On second thought, sit on the couch."

She rose and moved to the couch, dropping to edge.

He looked her over when he'd followed her. "Not like that. Lean back and lift your heels to the seat."

She leaned back, bending her knees and drawing them up against her.

He knelt in front of her. Catching her ankles he moved them out to either side of her and pushed her thighs wide until the lips of her sex parted moistly. She caught her breath when he leaned down to caress her sex with his mouth. The hot, faintly rough stroke of his tongue sent pleasurable jolts sizzling along her nerves. The heat of his mouth was divine as he covered her clit and sucked at the tender bud.

She gasped, slumping lower as he lifted her hips for better access, lathing her with an enthusiasm that sent her spiraling upward toward her peak in a breathless rush. She was teetering on the brink when he inserted a finger into her passage, stroking it and detonating the explosion that had been threatening.

Yveline's mind seemed almost to explode with the concussion of release, blackness crowding close. The spasms of rapture drew sharp, hoarse cries from her.

Spent, she sagged limply against the couch.

He allowed her a moment to rest and caught her hand, dragging her up from the couch. "Bedroom," he said succinctly, his voice faintly hoarse.

Still half drunk from the euphoria that had filled her, she led the way, wobbling slightly. He settled his hands on her hips, steadying her.

He joined her on the bed when she'd sprawled weakly on top of it.

She'd barely settled when he latched onto one puckered nipple and began to tug and pull on it with his mouth. Her belly clenched painfully, seeking his cock and finding nothing to cling to.

He remedied that. Shoving her legs apart and settling his hips between her thighs, he surged toward her at once. The head of his cock connected with her cleft and moved down to wedge itself firmly in the mouth of her sex. The second surge plowed through her resisting flesh and embedded him more deeply.

She gasped, lifting her hips to meet him when he thrust again, sucking in a sharp breath when he sank to her core.

Burying his face against the side of her neck, he set an agonizingly slow pace to begin with, teasing her, warming the embers of her passion until she was on fire again and clutching at him, bucking against him. "More Jake!" she demanded.

A shudder through him. Dragging in a harsh breath he set a faster, harder rhythm that drove them both quickly to the heights where they hovered for breathless moments before the deluge caught them and flung them into paradise.

Drifting afterwards in delight, Yveline stroked her hands over his body, exploring him thoroughly while he was too weak to resist.

He murmured a sound that might have been a complaint against her neck.

Finally, he rolled off of her and onto his side. Carrying her with him, he studied her face for a while. "I don' know how long it's gonna take Yvie, but I'm a determined man. When I set out to do something, I do it."

Yveline lifted a brow questioningly with a strenuous effort. "What, Jake?"

He dragged her against him and kissed her. "I've got t'cure this obsession I've developed for you. I'm sure, if I dedicate myself to it, I'll manage, eventually, to get my fill of you."

She sent him an expression that was half frown, half smile. "You think so?"

"I'm sure of it," he murmured, nuzzling her ear.

She shivered in delight. "How long, you think?"

"Years. A half dozen anyway."

The End

Underneath It All

By

Alicia Sparks

Chapter One

Shane turned over the coaster in his hand, staring blankly at the beer bottle label he had already peeled down to the glue. He couldn't believe he had taken this job. He hadn't even needed the money. But he did need the reward that would come at the end of the job.

When Johnny Hutchins called him two days ago to ask him to track down his sister, Shane felt that familiar stirring in his gut he had felt every time in the past few years when Emma Hutchins' name slid past someone's lips. He knew he had to find her, and he knew where she would be.

He had been reluctant to tell Johnny, the admirable younger brother, that his older sister was a high-paid stripper at *Escapades* down in South Louisiana. He had stumbled onto the news a few months ago and had time to deal with it. Part of him wanted to leave her there in her new life, but the other part knew he had to see for himself.

Emma had fled Honey Oaks for a damned good reason, and now it was time to bring her back home.

In a few seconds, she would be on stage, as Harley, the woman she pretended to be. He knew her inside and out, and he swore he would reclaim the woman who had gotten away from him so many times in the past. This time, he wouldn't let her slip away from him, dancing aside when he reached out to touch her. She did it to protect herself from him, from the place where she was born. Ever since they were kids, she was so much more than just his best friend's big sister. She was a woman who did not belong in the stilted town that had raised her. After her husband had died, she left town, hiding herself from the prying eyes of the small community, and Shane had not felt complete since she left.

The music started slowly. He raised his eyes from the bottle and focused on the stage. Whatever the deejay said didn't quite make its way into his brain as the woman with the long legs and the tightest ass he'd ever seen stepped onto the stage, her body covered with a long red dress, her ankles accented by the straps from her red high heels. Her long, dark hair was not naturally hers. Hers was a coppery red, reminding him of sex and how sex should feel.

Instantly, he thought of seeing those shoes tossed aside next to his bed, her long, red hair splayed out on his pillow. She would smile up at him, her eyes filled with honesty. He smirked at the thought. Emma was not known for being honest to very many people. She mostly lied to herself. Then again, what did a former cop know about honesty?

His work as a P.I. had proven to him that he couldn't always judge people by what they said or how they said it. Sometimes, their lies covered up a truth they couldn't admit. Other times, their lies covered up self-perceived flaws. Either way, there was sometimes a reason aside from manipulation that played a part in falsifying one's life. In Emma's case, it was mostly self-loathing that caused her to hide from her past and the life she had left behind in Honey Oaks.

It was self-loathing that also caused her to hide from him. For some reason, she couldn't admit to the sparks that flew between them every time they touched one another.

Their eyes locked and her lips turned up in a slight smile. She was cool, collected, eyeing him as if he were nothing more than another customer, here to throw bills at the stage and then jack off to her memory later on.

He tipped his cowboy hat in her direction and brought his beer to his lips. Sucking down the amber liquid, he imagined her tongue running over his body, waking up every nerve ending that had been dead for so long.

He held his breath as she turned her body, teasing him with her backside, bending over, showing him her soft, plump cunny beneath the red g-string as she slid her gown up to her lower back. Wiggling in front of him, she threw him a slight wink from between her legs.

When she rose up, her gown slipped back down to her feet and her hair flowed down her back. He longed to wind his fingers through her hair, to pull her close as she moved over him, that wild hair dancing in front of him.

"Hey, cowboy, you need another?" the cute waitress pressed her breasts together as she leaned in, filling his air with the sweet scent of roses and alcohol. God, he was hard. That damned woman on the stage had the power to do it to him every time.

"Make it two more."

"Don't plan to leave a hand free?" She smiled, her eyes teasing him as her tongue darted out to cover her lower lip.

"It's more fun when someone else lends a hand," he winked, sliding a twenty into her cleavage. "Keep the change."

"I'll be right back."

He didn't turn to look at her ass as she walked away. Instead, he met Emma's eyes, aware that she had watched the whole exchange. Jealousy flashed at him for a moment, letting him know she hadn't changed a bit in the five years since she'd been to Honey Oaks. Still wanted to be in charge, still wanted to call the shots, still wanted total control, which was all the same thing, when he stopped to think about it.

He raised his beer to her as she pressed her lips together in obvious annoyance before turning to flirt with the guy sitting next to the stage.

The club was near empty tonight, it being a Wednesday and not all that late yet. Dancers sat alone at tables scattered around the club, filing down their nails, talking to customers on cell phones and avoiding him. Three had approached him when he walked in, and all of them had been politely turned away.

He was here for one woman and one woman only. And right now, that woman was pulling her dress over her head and tossing it aside, revealing that shiny red g-string and matching lacy bra.

Her breasts pushed up in a pout, her nipples visible from beneath the flimsy material. He'd found heaven the night when she had let him touch her, when she had taken him into her body and made every wish he'd ever had come true.

He hadn't been able to forget her. Of course, his fascination with her had started the day he moved to Honey Oaks, a skinny kid with glasses and a longing to be a rodeo cowboy. He'd met that dream head on by the time he was twenty and had become a cop a year later, having grown weary of the rodeo life. He'd only touched Emma once.

"Here's your drink, honey. And if there's anything else I can do for you ..." the waitress let her voice trail off in obvious invitation as she lowered her lashes.

"Yeah, there is. You can tip her for me." He handed her another twenty, this time placing the money in her hand.

She smiled, disappointment shining in her eyes. He watched her walk away and place the money on the stage. Emma smiled at him before turning away, the money left on the stage when she disappeared behind the door to prepare for her second song.

With the stage empty and the deejay talking away about tipping the waitress, Shane finally remembered to breathe. God, that woman would be his undoing.

When the music started again, he had begun working on his third beer. The alcohol didn't dull the ache in his chest or the throbbing in his groin. He wanted her more than he'd realized. Coming here had been a mistake. He should have had the guts to tell Johnny he couldn't find Emma or the guts to tell him the truth. Anything other than coming to look for her himself.

True friend to the end. Johnny's wedding was three weeks away, and he had insisted on having his older sister there for the event. Shane knew deep down that he wouldn't disappoint Johnny. He only hoped that Emma felt the same way when he handed her the invitation and announced that he was taking her back home.

The song was a haze. Emma's white ensemble was a blur beneath the fog machine and soft throb of the black light, which caused her to glow. When she opened her bra, her breasts spilling forward, heaven before his eyes, his mouth went dry. He clutched his hand into a fist, hoping to restrain his growing need for her. Instead, it only worsened.

He remembered those breasts, bouncing gently above him as she rode him, her hair falling down her back, her pussy wrapped around him, pulling him into her. She called out his name, she touched herself, she opened her soul to him. Then she pulled on her jeans and walked away from him.

By the time he realized she had used him, he had already fallen in love with her. No other woman since her had been able to touch that part deep inside of him that Emma had brought to life when her fingers trailed down his body.

"You make me come to life," she had whispered into his ear as his cock entered her body.

Funny, she had killed him that night.

Chapter Two

"Careful, your weakness is showing."

He hadn't even realized she had walked out onto the floor, he was so wrapped up in images from that night. When she slid into the chair next to him, dropping her little black purse onto the table in front of her, he jumped in surprise.

Her voice was as smooth as whiskey as it purred from her throat. His was lost somewhere in his chest as her hand reached out to stroke his and her eyes turned down in wicked flirtation.

"Emma."

"It's Harley now. Has been for a while. Buy me a drink." She pulled a compact from her purse and began applying cherry red lipstick. He still hadn't moved.

"I'm here to …"

"Can I get a drink for the lady?" The waitress was back, now, her pert body not as enticing as it had been just minutes before.

"Yeah, uh …"

"Wine. Small bottle. Red, please," she ordered expertly.

"Sure thing, Harley."

"How much will that set me back?"

"For an old friend, it's a small price to pay."

"Old friend, eh?"

"Of course. I haven't forgotten you, you know."

"Then you might remember your brother, too."

"Johnny," her voice held a hint of nostalgia. "Is he okay?"

"He's getting married."

She smiled, her eyes lighting up at the news. Tossing her lipstick back into her bag, she let her back fall against the back of the chair and folded her arms across her chest. "Huh. How 'bout that. Who's the lucky girl?"

"Lynn Cummings from Wallace. Wedding's in three weeks."

"Let me guess. You are my escort." She ran her fingers along his jaw, teasing at his bottom lip for a second.

"Something like that." He shifted in his seat, his cock growing painfully uncomfortable beneath his jeans.

"You got the cuffs?"

"I'm not a cop anymore. Private investigator."

"What I always wanted. A Private Dick." Her hand fell to his leg, giving it a slight squeeze.

"Emma ..."

"Harley."

"Whatever."

"Am I moving too fast for you, cowboy? You always did take things too damned slow."

The waitress returned, causing Emma's hand to move from his lap just in time. He let go of the breath he had been holding as the woman placed the bottle of wine in front of him.

"Twenty dollars."

"Keep the change." He handed her a fifty, his eyes never leaving Emma's.

Damn the woman. In a matter of minutes, she had managed to turn him back into the gangly teen who couldn't talk to a girl ... a woman. She was most definitely a woman.

"Thanks for the drink. You're a big tipper." She poured the wine into a glass, downed the first glass and poured a second.

"And you're a big tease. Now drop the Harley routine and level with me."

"About what? My past? My present? My career choice?"

"That's a start."

"Mmmm. I got bored working at Hooters. Needed more excitement." She shrugged. "And you? You get bored working the beat, cuffing and frisking?"

"I got shot one too many times."

"You were shot?" Her eyes widened, the flirtation gone from her voice, her jaw set firmly.

"Yeah. Twice."

"God." She let out a deep breath. "I didn't know."

"You wouldn't. You've been gone a long damned time."

"Too long, I guess."

"My thoughts exactly."

"So, three weeks. I could do that."

"Even without the handcuffs?"

"Don't need handcuffs with a Private Dick," she winked.

Chapter Three

Emma ran her finger along the rim of her wineglass. Shane Richards. The one man who could bring her to her knees with a stare. She had managed to still the hammering of her heart and the nervousness that flew through her fingers when he had walked in. Now, she sat here, pretending he was nothing more than another customer, flirting, teasing, tempting the devil himself. And he was the devil incarnate with his cowboy hat, blue eyes and damned sexy smile. Not to mention those tight blue jeans.

It had taken more than a couple of drinks to get the courage to go to bed with him years earlier, but she had been smart enough to walk away before she spilled her guts to him and admitted how much she cared for him. To tell the truth, she'd carried a torch for him for longer than she'd have liked. He was everything she never wanted.

From his soft, southern drawl to his completely normal job, Shane was not for her. She needed excitement, adventure, the nightlife of the city. She needed to escape into another identity, to live a glamorous life. She did not need a country boy who was content to live on a farm and catch the bad guys for a living.

In Grant Parish, there weren't that many bad guys to be caught. Being a private detective was not all that exciting when one considered the pool of clients.

Still, her stomach quivered when she reached out to touch him, playfully teasing him. She had gone too far, though. Running her hand along his jeans, she remembered the night she had given herself to him. Seeing him naked had been a gift from the gods of beefcakes. Having him love her was heaven. Having him sitting next to her right now was a special kind of torture.

"Why are you here, Emma?"

"Why are you here?" She didn't want to admit to him all the reasons she felt more alive here than anywhere else. Well, almost anywhere else.

"To get you. Now, your turn."

"Well, it isn't to get you. I didn't come here so you would track me down a few years later. This has nothing to do with you."

"Glad to hear it. Don't need that on my conscience. So you'll come home with me?"

She almost spit out her wine. "Come home with you?" she managed as evenly as possible.

"Yes. Come back to Honey Oaks."

"I will. For the wedding."

"No. I mean now. For permanent."

"Why?" she let out a little laugh, the kind she usually uttered when she was nervous. Thinking of Shane and permanent was enough to make her stomach turn to jelly.

"Because your life is there."

"No, hon, it isn't. It's here. I'm quite happy." She raised the glass to her lips and let the liquid flow down her throat. It gave her a second to catch her breath, to think about what she should do, what she should say.

"You look incredible."

"So do you." She settled back into her chair, her nerves alleviating as he let out a slow smile.

"Glad to see you noticed."

"Same here."

"What time do you get off?"

"I don't know. When do you get off?" Flirting again. She *had* to stop doing that.

"As soon as I figure you out."

She opened her mouth to respond, but he had caught her in her own trap. This Shane seemed way more confident than the one she had slept with years earlier, and that one had been damned appealing.

Rather than responding, she ran her tongue along her bottom lip, a trick women used to make men think about sex.

"You got me, cowboy. So now, what are you gonna do?"

Playing the sex kitten with Shane should have been as easy as breathing. Instead, her heart hammered in her chest and her hands felt sweaty. Her life here was nice and private. Nobody ever knocked on her door without calling first and she was able to do exactly what she wanted without the fear of some nosy neighbor looking over her shoulder. Life in Honey Oaks was more complicated, even in its simplicity. There was always a façade to keep up, a pretense to uphold. And the last thing in the world she wanted was to become one of the desperate wives whose lives had been destroyed by the men they married.

No, she wouldn't go back to Honey Oaks. There was nothing for her there. She'd go back for the wedding, play the good older sister and then come back here, a place where she could blend into the crowd and virtually disappear.

"Tell me why you're still running." He raised his beer to his lips as if it were the most natural thing in the world, obviously unaware of how tempting she thought those lips were. If things were different … but they weren't. No need to fantasize about forever with a guy like Shane.

"I'm not running."

"Yeah, you are. It's not the end of the world, you know?"

"I don't wish to discuss my past with you."

"Everybody makes mistakes."

"Yeah, and nobody does it quite like I do."

He reached across the table, pulling her hands into his, forcing her to touch him. Staring down at his suntanned hand, she almost thought things could be normal for her. What did she know about normal? Her ex-husband had destroyed normal for her, and she hadn't even really liked him too much. If she allowed herself to really fall in love, she was bound to be doomed. And Shane was the type of guy a girl could lose herself in.

She pulled her hand away before she got too wrapped up in the moment.

"Nobody blames you." His eyes softened as he whispered, barely audible above the club's music.

"I blame me."

"Your ex-husband was insane. Nobody could have seen it coming."

"I slept with him every night. Do you know how it feels to be sleeping with a …"

"Don't, Emma. What he did is not your fault."

"Tell that to those kids' parents. He tortured them with his sick desires. Killing the man was too good for him."

"And he's rotting in hell now. There's no need for you to be there, too."

"I'm fine."

"No, you're not. You're ghost white just talking about him. You can't help it that he was a sick SOB with a taste for young kids."

"I should have stopped him."

"Come back with me. Don't let him keep you from the people who love you."

The deejay called her name, bringing her back to reality. Had Shane just told her he loved her? No. It wasn't possible. She was too complicated, had too much baggage for a guy like him.

"I have to go. It was nice to see you again." She stood and leaned across the table, brushing her lips against his cheek, which was slightly rough. "Take care of yourself."

He reached for her as she stepped away. She'd see him at the wedding. That was soon enough. Until then, she'd just think about how much she had screwed up her life and everyone else's and how she should have run off with Shane back when she'd had the chance.

Chapter Four

Shane had wondered what she could do to follow up the first set. Watching her earlier had forever burned the image of her body into his brain, as if it weren't already there. He got his answer when *Georgia on My Mind* began playing.

He felt his eyes glaze over a bit trying to keep up with the glow of her white teddy beneath the black lights. Again, she was getting under his skin. He felt the smoothness of her body in his mind, wondered how it would feel to touch her, to taste her. That was his destiny up there, in disguise, hiding her identity from the world, herself included. If only there were some way to convince her that she had nothing to do with her abusive ex-husband who had terrorized three kids before the cops took him out.

He knew Emma had to have felt the brunt of the man's abusive nature, too, though she never would admit to it. Instead, she left town, never to be heard from again. Sure, she sent an occasional card or letter, but she had once been so close to her family, he could hardly believe she would walk away like she did.

Then there was their relationship—hers and Shane's. After all these years, their one-night stand was the most profound relationship he'd had. He had loved Emma even before that night. Afterward, she held his soul in her hands. Her hurried marriage to Roger had been in a fit of anger when Shane announced he was joining the police force.

"You'll get yourself killed," she had pleaded.

"No, I won't. There's not much crime around here anyway."

"You don't know that. You never know who's

lurking around the corner."

She had been right about that. Roger had taken them all by surprise when they discovered he was a child molester.

Shane turned his attention back to the stage, watching her from beneath the brim of his cowboy hat. The urge to take her out of this place hit him hard, in the chest. Then he realized that was exactly what he had to do. By any means necessary.

A slow smile spread across his face. Emma was wild. Had been wild once upon a time. There was no way he was going to let her give up her life just because of her ex.

Shane had wanted Emma in that all-consuming, teenaged fashion ever since he had set eyes on her when he was fourteen years old. She had been sixteen and the closest thing to an angel he had ever seen. As luck would have it, the lanky guy he sat next to on the bus that first day in town had been her brother. A perfect situation. Until he had found out about her distaste for cowboys.

This didn't stop him from pining away after her in the lonely hours of the night for the next few years. When she graduated high school, she knew he existed, but only as her kid brother's best friend.

He was eighteen on the day he had decided to confess his love for her. No other woman he had met compared to her. And all of his attempts at teenage romance had failed because of his knack for thinking of Emma at the most inopportune times. Her family was having a barbecue the night before a big rodeo event. He swore that this would be the night. He would tell her how he felt, she would suddenly realize that he was a man, and all would be well with the world.

"Nice night," he had found her sitting alone on the front porch swing, waiting for the most recent in an endless string of college boys. Shane had that now or never feeling.

"Yeah," she didn't actually see him as he joined her, but the swing became heavy with the added weight.

"I'm glad you're here." His palms were sweaty. "I was hoping you would come to see us tomorrow."

"Oh, I'm not going to the rodeo," she smiled. "Luke is coming in and we're going to a concert. I'm sure you'll have a good time, though."

She was so casual, so cool. Couldn't she see he was dying here? He let his arm fall across the back of the swing. She was turned sideways and had her arm across the back also, giving him the opportunity to lay his hand on hers. As soon as their skin connected, she shot from the swing, completely unaware that he had touched her.

He watched her spring from the swing as her boyfriend's convertible pulled into the long driveway. He was her kid brother's best friend. And she was out of reach.

Not this time. This time, she was on stage, baring her body to a group of strangers, trying to case her pain in alcohol and strobe lights. He wouldn't think about the string of meaningless sex partners she probably had. Instead, he would focus on the woman, the one he once loved, the one who desperately needed to be saved from herself.

Chapter Five

Emma had already changed into her street clothes, determined to slip out the back of the club and avoid Shane. Taking off her dark wig and shaking out her natural red hair, she grabbed her bag and hauled it onto her shoulder.

"I'll be back tomorrow night," she told the deejay as he walked her to the door.

"Be careful, Harley."

"I will. I just have to go and clear my head."

"See you later." He stood at the backdoor, his arms folded as she unlocked her car and slid into the driver's seat.

She had explained to him as soon as she had left Shane's table that she had to go home to her own apartment. He was the manager on slow nights, like tonight, so it was his call in the end. Luckily, she had proven herself to be a loyal employee, so there was no danger of her not coming back.

Slipping her keys into the ignition, she started the car and took a look at herself in the rear view mirror. She hadn't been back to Honey Oaks since her life had fallen apart, thanks to Roger. Deep down, she knew she owed her brother the courtesy of going to his wedding, but she wasn't sure if she could face the crowd of people who would gasp when she entered the church.

Even if the town's scars had been healed, she would remind them all of what Roger had done. That was the last thing she wanted. She would never feel comfortable in a town where she reminded everyone of the worst possible thing to have happened there in the town's entire history.

"Get a hold of yourself," she managed. "It's all over." Her words didn't stop the tears that stung her eyes. She missed her family. There was an emptiness deep inside her that had been there since the day she left. She missed the quiet life she'd had in Honey Oaks. That life would never be hers again, though.

She and Shane had almost admitted their feelings for one another when he decided to join the police force of Honey Oaks, which was about six strong. The thought of being involved with a cop had scared the hell out of her. She'd known Roger from college and had called him up to vent her frustrations. The next thing she knew, he was promising forever and showing her how the two of them made sense together.

From that day forward, very little actually made sense. Then there had been the kids who had gone missing. For three days, the town searched frantically for them. When they found them, they had all been raped, and her dear, loving husband had been the one responsible for shattering their little lives.

She wiped the tears from her cheeks. Harley wouldn't cry, and Emma shouldn't either. The past should remain where it was, and Shane should go back to Honey Oaks without her.

Pulling her car out of the back parking lot, she eased out onto the highway. A black truck pulled out behind her, but she didn't pay much attention to it until it had followed her on the last three turns. A knot formed in her stomach as she glanced up at the rear view mirror. Someone was following her.

She'd heard so many stories of women being followed after work and she had been so careful to disguise herself and to park around back. Someone had obviously seen through her façade and was now tailing her.

The only thing she could make out from the truck's cab was a cowboy hat, and there was only one person who would know her no matter what kind of disguise she wore. As soon as the all night restaurant came into view, she turned on her blinker, inviting him to join her. Her past was refusing to stay in the past, so she had to find a way to force it into staying there.

She knew Shane well enough to know a few of his weaknesses. Every time the two of them had gotten close in the past, he had backed off, doing something stupid, like joining the force or not calling her for a week. Deep down, he was afraid of getting close to her. She could see it in his eyes. He was the type of guy who had more than commitment issues. He had issues with relationships in general.

That made two of them who'd never be normal. Constantly pulling people close only to push them away was a survival mechanism for people who had gone through what they had. He had lost his parents when he was young, and she had aided in destroying three kids. What a pair they made!

"I thought I'd buy you dinner," he explained as he stepped from the cab of his truck.

"Funny, I thought you looked like a stalker." She folded her arms and leaned against the car door.

"I wasn't through with our talk."

"I was. I can't go back there."

"Fine. But you don't have to shut out your family. Call them or something."

"I write." She raised her chin, defending herself against the man who looked at her as if he could see right through her.

"They love you and want you back."

"What about you, Shane? Do you love me and want me back?" She stepped toward him, wishing she had the confidence to pull off this ruse with him.

"You know I care about you." Her question obviously made him nervous. He had a certain manner about him when he got nervous. His usually confident stance dropped a bit and his eyes avoided hers.

"That's not what I asked, now is it?" She reached out

to touch him, noting the sharp intake of breath when her hands touched his shoulders.

"Emma."

"What? Stop? Please stop? Don't stop?"

"Come home with me."

"Why don't you come home with me first?" She braced herself for her next move. Snaking her hands around his neck, she pulled him into her and stood on her tiptoes, brushing her lips against his. She intended to keep the kiss chaste but to rub her body against him in such a way that would leave him running for the door.

Instead, he caught her, planting his hands on her ass, grinding her against him as his lips opened, taking hers into them, sliding his tongue into her mouth, sharing a piece of his soul with her. Her chest tightened. This wasn't supposed to happen. She was supposed to kiss him, and he was supposed to realize he was out of his league.

Instead, he opened up a raw need inside of her that she couldn't deny. It had been so long since a man had touched her, and then, the only man who had touched her had been lying to her. Even thinking about sex had seemed dirty since then. But having Shane's hands on her, feeling his heated breath enter her body made her realize how much she needed human contact.

God, she wanted him. She wanted to wrap herself up in his cowboy scent, eat him for dinner, then have him for breakfast. She wanted to lose herself in those blue eyes of his and never come up for air.

His hold on her ass loosened and he ran his hands up her back, pressing against her as they moved. The entire world stopped for a second while she got a hold of her senses. Then she managed to pull away from him. Stumbling back a bit, she knew he had beaten her at her own game.

Damn him, but he was smooth! He knew her weakness, and she was damned if she could do anything about it.

"Well?" he smiled.

"I thought we were having dinner."

"To hell with dinner. I want dessert."

Chapter Six

"No." She folded her arms and looked at him as if he had just asked her to rob a bank with him.

"What do you mean *no*?"

"I mean it's not that easy."

"You invited me to come to your place. You kissed me. Now, what are you trying to do?" He let his gaze linger on her face and realized he had pushed her too far.

"I'm trying to get rid of you." Wrapping her arms around her body, she turned away from him, avoiding his eyes.

"Why, Emma? You can't just kiss me like that and then tell me to go to hell."

"Why not?"

"Because you are right. I do care about you. More than you know. Seeing you tonight made me realize how much I need you in my life. Come home with me."

"I can't go back there."

"You have to. You have to go back and face everything. You have to realize nobody blames you." He reached out to touch her shoulder, but she pulled away. Making a fist and then slipping it into his pocket, he wished there were some way to take away her pain.

"Go away, Shane. Just go." He could hear the sobs in her voice.

"I won't leave you." Swallowing hard, he reached out to her, determined to hold her, determined to melt away her pain.

"It doesn't matter. I'm already dead. Can't you see that? Emma doesn't exist anymore. I'm Harley now."

When she turned to face him, all the sadness inside her struck him in the chest.

"No. You're not. You're just a scared little girl inside who needs my help. You need me to protect you from the world, honey, and I will."

"I don't need you. I don't need anybody at all."

"I don't believe you." By now, she had managed to back up to her car door. Trapping her with his arms, he placed them on either side of her body, making it impossible for her to escape.

"I don't care if you believe me or not. It's true. Now, please, forget you ever saw me."

"How can I forget? Damn you, I've been hard ever since you walked out on stage. I want you, Emma. But I want more than sex from you. I want all of you. Hell, woman, I love you. I always have, and I will do anything to save you from yourself."

"Then let me go," her lip trembled as she spoke, and her eyes glittered with unshed tears.

"Not yet. First, I'm going to show you how much I love you."

Her eyes widened as he reached into his pocket and pulled out his cell phone.

"What are you doing?"

"You'll see." He punched in the numbers and waited for the call to connect.

"Hello?" Johnny's voice picked up on the other end.

"Hey. You won't believe where I am right now."

"Where's that?"

"Standing in Baton Rouge. Talking to your sister."

Emma's mouth dropped open in protest as Johnny squealed with delight.

"He found her!" he shouted to whoever was with him. "Is she okay? When are you coming back?"

"We'll be back in two days. And she is fine. She can't wait to see you."

"Can I talk to her?"

He handed Emma the phone as she shook her head wildly in protest. "Talk to him," he whispered.

"Hello?" She placed the phone to her ear. "Yeah. I'm fine. It's good to talk to you, too. Congratulations on the wedding. Yeah. Of course. I wouldn't miss it for the world. Yeah. Two days. I love you, too. Bye."

She ended the call and pushed the phone into his hand before pushing past him to walk into the restaurant.

"So you're leaving with me?" he called behind her, rushing to catch up.

"I hate you, Shane Richards. I hope you rot in hell."

She pulled open the restaurant door then closed it quickly, not allowing him time to enter. He couldn't help the smile that spread across his face. So, he had been manipulative. She'd forgive him for that once she saw her family again and realized her life didn't have to end just because her ex was the devil incarnate.

Following her to the table, he allowed her the room to vent, to be mad, to get pissed off completely. He had won this round. She was going to go back home to see her family and see how much they needed her. While she was there, he planned to convince her how much he did love her and how much he needed her, too.

Chapter Seven

"So you've got me." Emma didn't look up as she stared at her menu, but the venom she felt was clear in her voice.

"I wasn't trying to trap you."

"Yeah, you were. Why else would you have called my brother? They don't serve beer here?" Tossing the menu aside, she folded her arms and glared at him.

"No beer. I have some at my hotel room, though. And I called your brother because he needed to hear from you."

She rolled her eyes at him as the waitress approached the table, then continued to glare as she stated her order, not looking at the waitress as she spoke. "Coffee, black, a diet soda and a burger all the way."

"I'll have the same. No diet soda, though. And fries." He passed the menus to the waitress and attempted to break through Emma's ice with his smile.

"You owe me."

"What do I owe you?"

At least now the frosty gaze had lightened a bit. It was replaced by the glow he remembered from their youth when Emma had an idea she wanted to try out on someone. "I won't go back home by myself. I'm not going to be someone for everyone to talk about, to pity. I need a ..." she stopped and let out a deep breath. "I need a date. For the wedding."

"A date? Do you really think that's necessary?"

"Yes, I do. A date will protect me from a lot of questions. It'll give me something to do, someone to talk to, someone to grab me by the elbow and lead me to the dance floor when things get a little too thick in the crowd."

"Makes sense," he shrugged, wondering where she was headed with this line of thought.

"Most importantly, I can't go alone because I don't want them to think I've been hiding myself from life for the past few years."

"Haven't you been?"

"No. I've been protecting myself, but that is neither here nor there. Outside, you said you loved me. I think you were just desperate to get me to go back home, but that isn't important either. You need to know that I cannot fall in love. There's no need to even play with the idea. I need a date, Shane, and since you're the only one I can trust …"

"Are you asking me out?" A slow smile spread across his face.

"I'm asking you to join me in an arrangement. Take me to my brother's wedding."

The waitress chose that moment to return with the food. "Here you go, kids."

"Thanks," Emma looked up at her and smiled.

"You can be sugary sweet when you want to," Shane folded his arms and leaned back in his chair, taking in her smile as the waitress walked away.

"When the moment fits," she shrugged and took a bite of her burger.

"I'll take you to the wedding. I'm going anyway."

"No. I don't want us to meet there. I want us to go together. As a couple."

"So you want us to pretend to be dating?"

"Something like that." She wiped ketchup from her lips with her napkin. Even though the move was not meant to be sensual, it sent a shiver of desire through him. He could almost feel her lips on him, feel her body pressed against him the way it had out in the parking lot.

Giving himself a mental shake, he vowed not to do this. He wouldn't have another weak moment with her. He'd already confessed his feelings for her, but now he had to back off and take things really slow with her. He knew her past affected her more than anyone realized.

"Okay. You lay down the rules, then. I'm game for whatever you have up your sleeve."

"I haven't decided on the rules yet. I've just now decided not to kick you in the shins under the table for calling my brother," she laughed.

The woman was a thousand contradictions. One minute, she was telling him how much she hated him, the next she was contemplating rules of a relationship, fake though it may be. And she got under his skin in a way he could never explain. Just the way she held her burger against her lips as she took a bite, then savored the flavor as if it were going straight to her soul. She didn't take life for granted anymore, which was why she hid herself from the world. As a detective, it was his job to read people, and he could read Emma. Their arrangement would be a safe way for her to return home, a safe way to keep herself hidden from the world while staying in plain view.

"It was good to hear his voice, though, wasn't it?" He straightened in his chair, taking another bite of his burger, the desire to reach across the table and take a bite out of her neck growing.

"Yeah, it was. Thanks."

"Are you thanking me? Sincerely? Not a hint of bullshit in there?"

"Yeah. I am. Don't get used to it."

"Wouldn't dream of it."

Chapter Eight

Emma closed the door to her apartment, wondering what the hell she thought she was doing. After all this time, her past was now staring her in the face and all she could think about was a way to get closer to Shane, the one thing from her past that didn't hurt nearly as bad as everything else. Her family had been kind to her during the ordeal with Roger, but they had to have been disappointed in her for not realizing her husband was a child molester.

The only person who had stood by her, making her smile, even if only temporarily was Shane, the one she had lost to be with Roger. She had lasted about two weeks after Roger's death. Then, she packed up, left home and never went back. Taking on a life as Harley gave her a new identity. Becoming a stripper put her in control of her body and her destiny. It was something few people would understand, but it was a way for her to protect herself from the outside world.

She dropped her keys onto the table by the door, slipped off her shoes and flipped on a light. Her apartment had always been enough for her. It was secure, roomy enough to hold all of her books and her CD collection, and it was private. No one here knew who she had once been or what she had been responsible for.

She padded through the living room, the wood floor cold against her bare feet. Picking up her remote control, she turned on the CD player, letting the soft music flow into the room. Wrapping her arms around herself, she let the music soothe her. Going home was going to be harder than she'd imagined. But now, she would have Shane by her side to help her through the rough spots.

"Nice place," his voice washed over her shoulder, brushing against her ear.

"It gets me by." She hadn't intended to invite him back to her place, but something about having him here made her realize how much she needed to be near someone.

"We don't have to do anything if you don't want to." His fingers were firm against her shoulder as they ran along her skin.

"I didn't invite you here to talk." She turned in his arms, placing her hands against his chest. "I invited you here to help me ease the pain. I know you have it in your chest, too, Shane. You feel as bad about Roger as I do. We're two of a kind."

"So you plan to use me for sex."

"If that's okay with you." Twining her fingers in his hair, she pulled his mouth down to hers, bracing herself for the passion-induced kiss she knew he would unleash on her. Tears welled up in her eyes when his breath blew into her body. With Shane, she could erase the pain, take it all away. Things could be the way they were before she had screwed up and married Roger.

"You're more to me than that," he whispered against her, breaking the kiss.

"I can't promise …"

"Shh … I don't need a promise."

He ran his finger along her bottom lip before replacing it with his lips. When his tongue delved into her mouth, his hands made their way down to her waist, raising her up and pressing her against him, his crotch hard, proof of his desire for her. She wanted him, too. There was no way she could deny how wet she felt having his hot hands on her. Part of it was the need to be touched. The rest of it was the need for him.

They stumbled against each other as they struggled to remove the tangle of clothes they were lost in. When her shirt hit the floor and his hands replaced her bra, cupping her breasts, she threw her head back in release. God, it felt so good to have him touch her.

"I love you," she thought she heard herself whisper, but couldn't be sure. She was lost in a sea of emotion. And she was completely beyond help.

"Emma, God, I love you," he groaned as he dipped his head toward her breast. He took it in his mouth, lavishly placing kisses around her nipple before taking it into his mouth. She arched her back, pressing her breast more fully against him.

His hand traced down her side, and she delighted in the shiver that went through her body at the contact. "Shane," she moaned as he lifted her, moving toward the sofa. "No, the bed," she managed, pointing the way to her room.

"Are you sure?"

"Yes. I need you."

He pushed open the door to her room, his arms strong around her as he moved. When he placed her on the bed, she spread her legs, inviting him into her embrace. God, how she wanted him! When his hands pressed against her thighs, she arched against him, waiting for him to touch her where she needed it most.

Finally, his fingers brushed against her vagina, softly stroking her lips. A shiver ran through her as she reached for him. Gently pushing her hand aside, he continued to tease her lips, running his fingers near her clit, but not quite touching her where she needed to feel his touch.

Her pussy grew wetter, clenching inside, hoping he would enter her soon. As he slid down her body, placing kisses on the insides of her thighs and down to her knees, his fingers moved to test her wetness.

"Oh, God, yes! Touch me there."

"I want to taste you," he breathed against her.

"Please taste me," she begged.

Finally, He dipped his hand between her thighs,

where she was wet and waiting for him.

He slid a finger into her, and she rewarded him with another moan. This was how a woman was supposed to feel. And making love was supposed to feel like this. His finger moved in and out of her, while she rocked against him.

"Shane," she moaned his name again.

"What do you want, Emma?" he moved above her, pressing his cock against her. "Tell me."

"I want you inside of me," she begged.

"No regrets?" He looked into her eyes as he spoke, a softness there glazed over with desire.

"No," she managed. "No regrets. Just love me."

He slid off of her long enough to slip on a condom, which he always kept in his wallet. When he moved back on top of her, his skin felt as if it were on fire. All he wanted to do was take her. Savagely. He wanted to make up for the wasted years. He wanted to burn an impression onto her that she would never forget. He wanted to make her his forever.

He slid inside of her and let out a moan when she opened for him. Hot, wet, soft. His body began to quake. If he lost it right now, he'd never forgive himself. She arched against him. "Be still," he warned.

"I want you. I want you to take me," she begged.

"I won't last long. God, you feel incredible."

"I don't care. I want you." She dragged her fingernails up his back, and that was his undoing.

He slid out of her and then pushed himself back in, all the way in. Their bodies molded to one another. She rocked against him again, threatening to milk him dry with the tremors that shook her body. She tightened around him, released him, tightened again. The whole time, she clung to him, her hands in his hair, her legs wrapped firmly around him.

He took her lips as he slid out and back in again. He wanted to take it slow, but when she bit his bottom lip, he let go. He pounded into her. She met his every motion. The headboard hit the wall. The pounding of the bed set the rhythm for them as he thrashed against her and she responded wildly, unleashing all the pain they had both felt for so long.

Shane felt his orgasm building as her sweet cunt spasmed around him, the waves washing over him. She quaked beneath him, her muscles tensing and releasing. As he shot his seed into her, she arched against him, grinding against her labia.

"I'll keep you safe," he whispered against her, brushing her hair off her face.

"I need you to do that for me."

Chapter Nine

Mars Hill Church, the only building in the area, was ten minutes down bumpy dirt roads in a stretch of no-name land. It should have taken five minutes to get there, but that was before Shane pulled over onto a side road and killed the engine. Emma's stomach did a little flip-flop and she carefully examined her nails, feigning lack of interest.

Shane turned in his seat to face her. "I'm glad you're here."

"I'm nervous." She shifted in her seat so that the door was to her back.

"I know. But this will be fine. You'll see." He shifted too, so they were facing each other.

The usual twinkle was gone from his eyes, having been replaced with a mask of seriousness. "Okay," the word was barely a whisper. She hadn't realized how the nearness had affected her. She felt enveloped by all things Shane. The car had his scent: leather, sweat, man. And the effect on her nerves was intoxicating.

"I want to talk about what happened between us in Baton Rouge." He looked her straight in the eyes as he spoke.

"We both know what happened," she turned her head to avoid his gaze.

"Yes, but we need to talk about it." He reached out to push aside a stray hair from her cheek. The contact of his hand against her skin sent a shiver through her. The past few weeks had been filled with nervousness over going back home, but it had also been filled with thoughts about their night together. He had been so caring, so gentle, so much of everything she had needed.

Now, she wanted more.

"So, talk." Being close to him was making it hard to think, hard to breathe.

"I want …" he stopped, raked a hand through his hair.

"You want?" Her stomach flipped over, the butterflies having a frenzy in there.

"I want us to be friends. Real friends. I want you to know you can lean on me."

"I do know."

"Then don't hide yourself from me. Let me take away your pain. Let me be there for you."

"It's hard to trust."

"I know. But you can lean on me."

"Thanks." She squeezed his hand.

"I think that deserves more than a handshake, don't you?" he smiled, his eyes lighting up with mischief.

"You have always known how to make me laugh."

"Good. Hold onto that. And you have to know that things will be fine with your family. I promise. They are dying to see you."

As he turned to start the car again, he placed his hand on hers, leaving it there for the remainder of the drive. It was more than a comfort having him here with her. It was everything she needed.

* * * *

"Emma!!!" the bundle of energy could only be one person: Kelly. She came running down the aisle, ignoring the fact that the minister was trying to get everyone to sit down so the ceremony could begin.

"Kelly," Emma held her breath as her sister squeezed the life out of her. "It's good to see you," she gave Kelly one last squeeze. "We should sit down."

"Lynn's in there crying her brains out. It'll be a while yet," she linked arms with Emma.

"Why's she crying?"

"Oh, you know. Something Mom said. She has a knack," Kelly rolled her eyes. "Hey, Shane," she crooned, looking over Emma's shoulder.

"Hi, Kelly," he sang back. "When are you gonna run away with me?"

"When you decide to give me that car of yours," she winked at Emma. "Come, let's sit. By the way, I love the dress." She clasped Emma's hand and led her to the front pew.

Kelly had always been the active one, and she was more beautiful now than Emma had remembered. Fitting the casual theme, her jeans clung to her curvy body and her chestnut hair swirled around the thick black belt at her waist. Emma felt overdressed.

"I'm so nervous," Emma said, taking her place beside Kelly. "Where is everyone?"

"Well, Mom is in there with the bride making her presence known and Dad and Kevin are with Johnny. Oh, and Brenda's handling a food crisis. We're all accounted for," she smiled. "I'm glad you're here. Maybe you can run interference tonight."

"Don't count on it," she rolled her eyes, unable to deny how easy it was to slide back in to the family she had abandoned. Kelly squeezed her hand, her way of assuring Emma that things were going to be okay. She glanced sideways at Shane who sat on the other side of her, the picture of support.

"You ok?" Kelly clung to her arm.

"Yeah, I'm fine. Just a little overwhelmed. I've been in less than an hour, you know."

"I know," Kelly squeezed her hand. "What's up with you and Shane?" she whispered.

"He's my date," she whispered back as Shane placed his arm on the back of the pew, assuring her he would be there for her. This was too much like a fairytale, and she was afraid she would wake up to find that she was still in Baton Rouge, or worse, still married to Roger.

"Here they come," Kelly whispered.

Johnny looked nervous. He was wearing khaki colored slacks and a light blue polo shirt. His face was a mixture of sobriety and tension. He looked so young to Emma even though he was twenty-eight. Kevin followed behind him wearing black jeans and a gray shirt. He winked at Emma when he saw her. His dark hair was cut short and he was the only one of the three not wearing a cowboy hat. At twenty-two, he was at least three inches taller than Johnny. Jack was dressed similar to Kevin, and he left the altar to quickly hug his daughters.

Emma watched as Lynn's mother was escorted in by Lance, a childhood friend of her brother. They were followed by Emma's mother who, instead of sitting with her daughters, sat in the second row at the end with her new husband. She waved to Emma very discreetly as she slid into the pew and then gave her a hug before sitting. Emma was immediately enveloped with the scent of vanilla. It reminded her of the way things used to be.

Lynn was beautiful, Emma decided, upon seeing her in her Sunday best. She had chosen a simple beige colored sweater and a black and beige flowered skirt. Her classic white skin and very little makeup added to her beautiful simplicity. Her red blonde hair hung in ringlets around her face making her look angelic. Perfect. She was perfect for Johnny. He was the sensitive one, the stable one. And Lynn was exactly what Emma would have pictured for him.

Emma listened to the vows as they were being spoken and watched the way Johnny ran his finger along the back of Lynn's hand to soothe her. She could tell that they loved each other and was suddenly envious of the emotion displayed on their faces. Something pulled at her chest, urging her to turn around. When she did, she and Shane locked eyes. They held one another for longer than she would have liked before she finally turned away. A flood of emotions washed over her as Johnny recited the words to the country song, "I Can Love You Like That."

Shane's arm around her shoulder kept her tears in check. She could get through this without crying, and she could face the after wedding events, too. Watching as the bride and groom exited the church, she was anxious for what she knew was to come. It was time to face the rest of her family.

Shane guided her out the door and kept his hand on her back as they joined the congratulations line.

"Not thinking of sneaking out are you?" Emma jumped at the sound of her brother's voice.

"I wouldn't dream of it," she tearfully threw her arms around Kevin.

"Hey now, the hair," he patted his head, pretending to smooth down the closely cropped 'do.

"It's good to see you," she gave him one last squeeze before releasing him.

"You too. Come on, we've got to go say our hellos and stuff," he linked his Emma's arm into his.

"There's my favorite big sister," Johnny lifted Emma off of her feet. "It's good to see you."

"You too," she smiled. "You looked so handsome up there," she ran a hand along his cheek, which he promptly took and placed against his lips.

"You look pretty good yourself. Have you seen Mom yet?"

"I saw her come in, but I haven't seen her since." Their mom was known for avoiding crowds. "Congratulations, Lynn," Emma squeezed her new sister-in-law.

"Thank you," Lynn's eyes were red from crying. She clung to Emma for a few seconds before releasing her.

"I'm gonna go find Dad," Emma smiled.

"He's driving Brenda back out to the house to get her car so she can go on to Lynn's parents," Johnny shrugged.

"I'm going to get some air, then." Anything to get away from the drawing crowd. As everyone began exiting the church, the crush of people and familiar faces from the past made her feel as if she were in a fun house.

Thankfully, the reception hall just across from the church was completely empty. No self-respecting Southerner would actually hold a reception here. It was reserved for family reunions, baby showers and Sunday school classes. But it was the perfect place to hide out from the questions that Emma wasn't quite ready to face.

She sighed, ran her hand along the wall until she found the light switch. This had all seemed like such a good idea. She would come home, go to the wedding, stay here for a while. It was a nice, neat plan. And within two minutes it had come crashing down. She hadn't even had a chance to prepare for the flood of feelings that she'd felt upon seeing everyone again.

Every teenager she looked at seemed to be a haunting face of one of the kids Roger had brutalized. Every mother could have been one who had lost her heart when her child was abducted. Thankfully, the children had been returned "in tact" as some said. No one knew the extent of damage Roger had done aside from the obvious physical wounds.

Shaking the thought from her head, she turned when she heard the door open and close behind her. She didn't even have to turn around to know who would be standing there.

"I thought I'd find you in here."

"And what made you think that?" she turned to face him, wishing that she hadn't. He was breathtaking. He looked like one of those romance novel cowboys or something. He made it hard to ignore the way her blood seemed to quicken any time he was near.

"It's your nature, ain't it? Sneak out when the crowd becomes too thick," he ran a hand along the Sunday School table near the door.

"You don't know anything about my nature," she folded her arms, silently cursing him for being dead on.

"I know you're damned stubborn." He reached out to touch a curl that had fallen into her eyes.

"What are you doing?" she pulled away at the slightest contact with his skin.

"Your hair. It … uh … fell a little."

"Well, it's fine now," she backed away from him, knowing instinctively that he would follow her.

"You don't have to hide from me. I know this is hard for you."

"I'm sorry. I don't mean to be so … whatever I'm being."

"Bitchy?" he smiled.

"Yeah. That."

"No problem. I have tough skin."

They both jumped when the door swung open again. Kelly came bounding in. "They need you," she cried, almost out of breath.

"Who?" They asked in unison, feeling like two kids who had just been busted.

"The photographer. Come on," without waiting for a response, Kelly grabbed her sister's hand and pulled her away, the tension between herself and Shane lost in the chaos.

"There she is," Johnny called out. "Hey, Sis. Where were you hiding?"

"Next door," Kelly offered.

"How's my girl?" Her dad pulled her to him, obviously glad to see her after so long. She felt terrible for having been away for so long, but at least she had come back. Thanks to Shane.

"I'm fine," she hugged him, glad to be in her dad's safe embrace after so long.

"How was the trip?"

"Okay." She took her place in the photos.

Kevin took the opportunity in between flashes to lock Emma into a bear hug. Then he turned to Kelly, "I got hooch in the car."

"Thank Gawd," she smiled. "Don't know what I'd do without you bro."

"Hey you're not driving tonight are you?" Jack Farrell knew his kids well enough to know that they'd say, no, dad, we're not driving and then do it anyway. Still, he had to ask.

"No, Dad," they chimed in together.

"So, how are you?" her dad slid his arm around her shoulder.

"I'm good. I'll be fine."

"It's good to have you back. I hope you'll stay a while."

"I will. It's good to be back," she managed, hoping she could hold back the tears a bit longer, not wanting to ruin her make up.

Chapter Ten

"We'll see you at the house, right?" Johnny asked, as if he were afraid Emma wouldn't go to the reception.

"I'll be there," she planted a fake smile on her lips.

"Good. Cause I only plan to do this once. And I want you there, okay?" he bent his forehead in her direction, scolding her with his eyes.

"I'll be there," she promised.

"I'll make sure of it," Shane stepped forward and placed his arm around Emma's shoulder.

"Thanks, Shane, you're a good guy," Johnny slapped him on the shoulder and then gave Emma a quick kiss. "See you there."

"Sure thing."

Emma watched Johnny take his new bride by the hand and lead her out of the church. She and Shane were the only ones left now. "Churches are such strange places," he commented, twirling the stem of a flower between his fingers before holding it out to her.

"Yeah, I guess," she took the rose from his hand and brought it to her nose. "Everyone comes here to celebrate the start of something or the end of something. But very few come here in between."

"You getting all philosophical on me?" He stepped toward her, a devilish smile on his lips.

"No. I was just saying …"

He squeezed her shoulders, inhaled sharply and then let go. "Come on. We need to go."

"Thank you, Shane. For making me come here to face my demons."

"There's still a lot to face. I'm here with you, though."

"You're too good." She swallowed hard as her

tongue darted out to run along her bottom lip. Sometime in the past few weeks, during all of her daydreams about Shane and her memories of making love to him, she had come to need him more than she'd like to admit.

"It's good to have you home."

Home. She was home. And that pain in her stomach that had begun this morning as soon as she had driven through Lafayette was getting to be a real bother. It felt like there was a hole there; one that needed to be filled. And she couldn't believe she had ended up back here in an attempt to fill it. What had she been thinking? This was the place where everything had gone wrong.

"We're gonna be late," she managed.

"Yeah. Come on."

* * * *

"You're quiet," he commented as he pulled into the driveway of the Miller's home. It was one of those long, country driveways, the kind that looks like a dirt road but really is a dead end. It was lined on both sides by ancient pine trees.

"Just thinking," she turned and gave him a slight smile.

"Oh? Wondering how to get me to dance with you?"

"No wondering how I'm supposed to survive a party with all the townspeople there."

"You'll be fine. You have a hell of a date, remember?"

"I know. Thanks. Again."

"Your brother is my best friend. I would do anything for him. Finding you was just icing on the cake." He squeezed her hand as he stopped the car in the Miller's yard.

If there was alcohol anywhere in the house, Emma would find it. She needed a glass of wine or something to take the edge off. Shane had managed to wear down her defenses in the five minutes they had been alone. She'd never be able to handle dancing with him.

Making her way through the crowd, she found the bar and ordered a glass of wine before attempting to disappear into the mix.

"Dance with me," a delightful shiver went up her spine at the sound of his sultry voice. Emma turned, knowing Shane was standing so close to her that they would practically be touching.

"Don't know if I can." She felt the edge of the table sharp against her backside, but if she moved away from it, she would be standing too near him. She held her glass of wine between them as if it were strong enough to break the spell he had cast over her.

"I'll show you how," he murmured, making the words sound way too seductive. He took her glass from her hand and placed it on the table, sending a shock wave through her body at the slightest contact with her fingers. "No one's watching," he took her in his arms before she could protest and managed to maneuver her away from the table.

"That's not fair," she placed a hand on his chest to keep breathing space in between them.

"What? Me dancing with you?"

"No. You making it feel awkward for me to refuse you." She closed her eyes as he pulled her into his arms and every muscle in her body melted upon contact.

"There you go using those big words on me again. My poor country soul can't take it," he smiled. "Now shut up and dance with me," he gently, yet purposefully, moved her invading arm so that they were chest-to-chest.

"You wear that hat to hide your horns?" she couldn't resist resting her head on his chest. If she was going to be forced to dance with him, she may as well burn the memory into her brain. It may be the last chance she got to live in a fantasy world where cowboys had hearts of gold.

"Don't you know the devil is a cowboy?" he

chuckled. She relaxed against him, comforted in how good he felt.

"I knew he had blue eyes and blue jeans," she managed.

"You know your classic country music."

"I grew up here, remember."

"Yeah," the wistful sound of his voice wasn't lost on her.

Emma tried to block out all of her thoughts and just enjoy the moment, but she couldn't block out what she knew to be true. She and Shane had made love. And she was desperately close to falling for him even as her past threatened to control her every move.

Being near him made the very act of breathing painful, but she was determined not to let go of him just yet. Emma gave herself up to the music for a minute. It was a special occasion, she decided. So, she closed her eyes and let herself imagine that she and Shane were alone. That the past did not matter. But the tug in her heart wouldn't allow the fantasy to continue. Her chest ached as she pulled away from him.

"I have to sit down," she turned her face from his, not wanting to look into those eyes of his. To say she could drown in those oceans seemed too cliché, but it was the truth. Every time she looked into them, she lost herself.

"I'll sit with you," he offered, seizing her arm so she couldn't escape.

"No. You dance. I'm sure your card is full." She shook her head, pulling away from his offending arm.

"Not tonight," his face softened as he spoke, but he released his hold on her arm and let her slip away.

"I'll be back. I need to find a restroom."

"Are you okay?"

"I'm fine. I just need a minute."

He watched her as she walked away, feeling his heart break a little with each step she took. How the hell had he gotten himself into this mess? He was over Emma

Farrell. Had been for years. Well, months anyway. Hell, he had never been over her. If he had, he wouldn't have tracked her down and convinced her to come back home. And he wouldn't have made love to her even though he knew she was just using him to dull the pain.

"You love her, don't you?"

"What?" he spun to see Kelly standing there, hands on hips.

"I said you love my sister," she poked a finger into his chest.

"No, I don't," he swiped at her hand.

"Then what's with those steamy looks between the two of you?" She gave him a light punch on the arm.

"Maybe you should talk to her," he rubbed his arm. For a tiny thing, she sure was strong.

"Why? Do you know something I don't? Emma's not like us," she said. "So you'll do well to remember that."

"Are you threatening me, Kelly?"

"You bet I am," she punched a finger into his chest again for effect.

"All I know is that she's here now, and she's got a lot to deal with."

"And you remind her of the past."

"Everything reminds her of the past, Kelly. She still hurts in a way you and I will never understand."

"I know. I'm sorry. Thanks, Shane. You know, for bringing her back."

"I just hope I can keep her here."

Chapter Eleven

"There you are," Shane had been looking all over for her and finally found her on the porch swing. "Want to dance?"

"I don't know if I can go back in there." Tears sparkled in her eyes as she looked up at him.

"What happened?"

"Nothing happened. I just feel like a freak in there."

"It's because you won't let go of the past. No one here blames you."

"I know you keep saying that, but I'm not sure if I believe you."

"Trust me."

"Where are the kids now? The ones who …"

"They're all gone. Moved out not long after you left. Too many bad memories."

"So their families are gone?"

"Yes. Most of them. The parents are gone. A few aunts and uncles here and there."

"I didn't realize. I guess I just thought …"

"You thought time stood still here."

"Yeah. I guess I did."

"So what are you so afraid of?"

"I'm not afraid of anything. Nothing specific anyway," she folded her arms in front of her chest and avoided his eyes.

"Then dance with me."

"You're not afraid I'll step on your toes?"

"Do it if you want to. I won't be able to walk for a week," he mumbled. "Just dance with me."

"Shane, I didn't come here to get close to you," she avoided his eyes as she spoke even though she was curious if she'd made an impact with her words.

"I know that," he clasped his hands in his lap, the safest place for them.

"Then why do you insist on being close to me?" Why won't you just leave me alone? She wanted to shout at him, rave at him. Instead, she swallowed really hard, knowing her anger was unfounded. She was afraid of everything, and he knew it, which was why it was so difficult to be with him. He was everything she needed and couldn't have.

"I guess it's a gift," he flashed a crooked grin in her direction. "Tell me something, Emma. Do you care about me at all?"

The question wasn't what she'd expected, and she had to admit that he caught her by surprise. She straightened and took in a deep breath and then let it out slowly. "You know I do."

Shane looked out over the scene before them. It could have been their wedding. The night was perfect enough for fairytales to come true. "You know," he started, not facing her at first and then slowly turning toward her, "I would have walked to Baton Rouge barefoot if I thought it would have stopped you."

"Shane, please," her voice shook a bit. She had known that he would be her downfall. She had only hoped to hold onto her sanity for a few more days.

"What, Emma?" he whispered. "What do you want?"

Emma straightened, about to speak when Johnny intervened.

"Hey, can I barge in," Johnny had noticed the two of them sitting on the swing and had noticed a change in Emma's demeanor.

"Hey, Johnny, I'd love to," she stood before he had the chance to make the offer. He shrugged at Shane as Emma led him off.

"In an awful hurry to get away from him," Johnny laughed as he took his sister in his arms to the tune of some sappy Garth Brooks song.

"No. I just wanted to dance with my little brother,"

she smiled.

"That's younger brother," he reminded her that he was well over six feet tall, and she had barely broken five feet.

"Whatever," she rolled her eyes at the constant teasing she had received about her height.

"You seem distracted. You sure that good-for-nothing cowboy wasn't bothering you?"

"I'm sure. He just doesn't know when to let things lie." His words echoed in her head. *Would have walked barefoot to Baton Rouge.*

"I see. And what kinds of things should he let lie?" Johnny's eyebrows raised.

"Nothing important. Now let's dance." She waved off the worried expression on his face, ignoring those puppy dog eyes that always could force the truth out of her.

"Not so fast," he slowed his pace even further so they had almost stopped moving altogether. "Something is wrong. I can see it in your eyes."

She narrowed her eyes at him. Johnny had always been the one who could read her like a book. "I don't want to ruin your night."

"You won't. Nothing can ruin tonight. I'm married. You're back where you belong. Life is good."

"But it's not. I can't forget the past."

"We've all moved on here. We wish we could have done it with you. Everyone knows why you left. We understand the pain, but you can't let it control you, Emma. You're smarter than that. And Shane cares a hell of a lot about you."

"What has he told you about me?"

"Nothing. I can see it in his eyes. He's been waiting for you all these years."

"I doubt that."

"He got you here, didn't he? He swore he would find you, and he did. And now you are back where you belong."

Johnny was just being nice, but those last words haunted her well into the night. *Back where you belong.* The problem was Emma didn't belong here.

* * * *

"So you going to the barbecue tomorrow?" Kevin shuffled through the CDs, as he was playing deejay tonight.

"No. I have to be somewhere," Emma lied.

"Damn shame. Shane knows how to throw one."

"I'm sure he does," she couldn't help but glance at the swaying bodies. Shane was cozied up to Lindsay Mitchell in a nice, slow dance, causing jealousy to course through her.

"Got a pool and everything," he waggled his eyebrows. "I'm sure there'll be plenty of hunnies there."

"I'm sure," she tried to ignore that feeling deep in the pit of her chest. "When did Shane get a pool?" she finally asked after realizing Kevin was watching her watch Shane.

"Last summer. Been wanting to do it for a while. He's got one of those big inground pools with a deck and a waterslide. Off to one side there's a hot tub. It's real nice."

"Must've cost a fortune," she turned away from the dance floor now, unable to watch any longer.

"Yeah, but he's got plenty. He's into racehorses now, you know," he switched out the CDs and put on another slow country song.

"I thought he was a detective," she flipped through the CDs. "I never was one for country music."

"That's about all we've got. Unless you're into karaoke. You know, *I Will Survive*," he did his best disco interpretation.

"That's quite all right," she groaned.

"Your boy Shane is loaded."

"You mean drunk?" she sipped her punch, trying to look at Shane without being obvious.

"No. I mean rich. Sold a racehorse last summer for a million dollars."

"You're kidding." Emma didn't realize racehorses were so expensive.

"I never kid about money," he took a swig of his beer and set it back down. "Yep. Some guy in Dallas. He up and decided one day he wanted a racehorse, so he contacted the track and they set him up with Claudia, she runs Shane's Arkansas ranch. Anyway, the guy goes and gets the horse and brings it home. He has no place to put the thing, so he ties it to a tree in the front yard as a present for his wife. Funny thing is, when the wife drove up, the car scared the horse, the horse bucked and broke his neck." He made a whistling noise, "one million dollars down the tubes."

"That's terrible," she suppressed a giggle.

"Yeah. Shane replaced it with one worth half a million. Felt guilty about the whole thing. The guy has bought three more since."

"So he has a ranch in Arkansas, too?" it was more of a statement of wonder than a question.

"Yeah. Long story there, but he doesn't really run it so much as own it. Claudia is pretty capable. And she's a hottie."

"How did Shane get into racehorses? Where did he get that kind of money?"

"Inheritance. From his grandfather."

"I had heard he'd passed away."

"Yeah. They were real close. Will this do?" he handed Emma a CD.

"Guns n Roses?" she wrinkled her nose.

"Yeah, it's all I could come up with. What's that slow song, *Patience*?"

"Yeah, that's it."

"Don't say I never did you nothing."

"Believe me," she laughed, "I'll never say that."

Chapter Twelve

"Where are you staying tonight?" Shane slid his arm around Emma, pulling her close to him, avoiding asking the real question. *Will you stay with me tonight?*

"I hadn't thought that far ahead, to tell the truth."

"Oh. I thought you came here with a plan. You seem to always have one."

"Shows how much you know. I rarely ever know what the hell I'm doing."

"You made the right choice coming here tonight."

"I'm glad you think so. I'm still not convinced. My stomach is a big knot."

"Wanna dance again?" He was itching to have her in his arms, having thought of little else all night. Emma had a lot to deal with, but he really wanted to be on her list of priorities.

"It's getting late. I suppose I should think about where I'm staying," she shrugged away from him, obviously avoiding his gaze.

He cleared his throat, "I'm sure your dad will want you at home."

"No doubt."

"Stay with me." The words fell out before he could stop himself.

"What?"

"You heard me. Stay with me. Tonight. I can tell you're still not sure about being here. Nobody has mentioned the past to you. Now you have to let go of it."

"I don't know if I can."

"I am willing to help you. I'll do whatever it takes. You know I will."

"Some scars don't heal as easily as others."

"And some only heal when you stop picking at them." He tipped her face toward him, forcing her to look him in the eyes. Once again, they glittered with tears. "I know this is hard for you."

"You have no idea."

"I have some idea. When you left, I felt empty inside. I knew you were hurting, but I also knew you needed time to heal. I just let you stay away too long."

"So it's your fault I've been gone?" she smiled.

"Yeah. Partly. Come home with me tonight."

"Aren't you throwing a party tomorrow?"

"You'll already be there, then."

"I can't this time. I have to think. Being near you makes it hard to think."

"Then don't think. Just feel." Taking her hand, he placed it on his chest, feeling the heat from her radiating out to him.

"I don't deserve to be happy."

"No one deserves it more than you do." He ducked his head down to place a tiny kiss on her lips, but on contact, he exploded into a fiery storm of desire. When she sighed against him, opening her mouth for him, he pulled her close, oblivious to the room full of people around them. She had wanted him here as her date. Well, she got more than she bargained for because he planned to be more than that.

"Shane," she whispered against him.

"Yeah?"

"Take me home."

"I need you, Emma. I need you to make my life complete. I've had a hole inside of me ever since you left. And I need you back. I need you here," he put her hand over his heart to emphasize the point. "I need you here."

"I'm here, Shane. But I can't promise anything more than tonight."

He pulled her to him. He'd die without her. She was

the only woman he'd ever loved. He had spent most of his life trying to find a way to be with her. And now she was here, and she was his. "I love you, Emma, and I'll take what I can get from you."

"I love you, too, Shane. I think I always have, but things are complicated."

He laughed, "I know they are. Now be quiet." He covered her lips with his, drinking her in, ignoring the sounds of the reception around them.

Chapter Thirteen

Shane wanted to wait. He wanted to sweep her into his arms and carry her to his bed. Love her in the place where he had dreamt about her forever. But when they walked in the door, she clung to him, molding against him, breathing life into him. He was afraid that if he let her go, she'd have time to think, to come up with some new reason why she didn't need him. She would realize that was better than him after all. He didn't hesitate as he buried his head in her hair, drinking in her scent.

"Love me," she whispered into his ear.

"I do love you," he whispered, coming up to capture her lips again. Raw emotion flooded him. He would swear that his heart was breaking, the pain was so intense. Then he realized that he was alive for the first time in his whole life. It was like his heart was beating after being brought back from death. Kick-started by the fiery redhead who was pulling him back down on top of her.

He entered her mouth, explored, trying to feed his hunger for her. Her lips yielded, opening, giving him more, more. His tongue darted in and out searching for that hidden part of her deep inside her mouth. She quivered against him, longing to feel him inside of her.

He lifted her, carrying her to the rug by the fireplace. This time, he swore he wouldn't let her walk out on him. He would fight to the death if need be. She would not leave him again.

Slowly, he slid out of his jeans and inhaled sharply as her hand slid down his chest, stopping just below his navel. Her eyes searched his for permission. He smiled down at her, encouraging her to proceed with her exploration of his body. God, he was going to die! He felt it as surely as anything he had ever felt when she wrapped her fingers around him. This was heaven.

He tried to remain still and calm as she continued to move. "Emma," he groaned when she finally moved down to capture him with her mouth. He hadn't expected this. The intensity of the feeling sent spasms throughout his body. He threw his head back, unable to control himself. He wanted to make her stop. The feeling was so intense. In one motion, he moved her onto her back. She looked up at him, her eyes cloudy with passion. "I love you," he whispered as he slipped into her.

Chapter Fourteen

Emma managed to make it through the barbecue the next day without anyone mentioning her staying with Shane the night before. Nobody even seemed to remember the evil Roger had done. If they did, they certainly didn't mention it to her. Life in Honey Oaks seemed to be nothing other than normal.

Why couldn't she let go of the past then? She had admitted that she loved Shane, and he loved her, but she wasn't sure if she deserved this life. Being a dancer, masquerading as Harley had been liberating. She had been here for three days, and Shane hadn't even mentioned her other job or other life. She couldn't stay here forever, though. There were rules about women like her, people whose poor character judgment placed others in danger.

"I want you to stay here with me," Shane's fingers wound around hers as they lay in bed, tangled up with one another once more.

Emma's first thought was to turn down the offer. She straightened. "I'll stay," she said finally, hoping he didn't see the hesitation in her eyes.

The first day and night were spent in bed. Not that she'd slept that much. She didn't realize how difficult it was going to be just to be back home, still surrounded with doubts.

She pulled herself out of the empty bed, her stomach protesting the movement. She went to the kitchen, deciding that maybe she was just hungry. A smile crossed her lips. She and Shane hadn't exactly eaten much the past couple of days. Shane had left a note for her on the fridge. *There's veggie stuff in the freezer. Hope you feel better. S.*

The "veggie stuff" turned out to be vegetarian sausage. Too strong for her stomach, so she settled for coffee and toast. After eating, she stepped out of the house and headed for the corral, which she could see from the kitchen window.

Emma tried to hide her fascination with him as he approached the wooden fence that surrounded the small training corral. Lean, muscular, tanned. She watched the sweat rolling down his bare chest and had to force her eyes up to meet his. It wasn't the first time she had seen him shirtless, but she was still amazed at the raw power beneath those t-shirts he usually wore. And she was fascinated by the battle scars that were scattered across his taut flesh.

A scar from a puncture wound fell just below his rib cage on the left side. A bull's horn, she guessed. His right shoulder carried marks from another, and a thin, long scar ran across his heart. He'd been badly hurt in a rodeo over a year ago. Some kind of benefit he had done. Here was the proof. None of the marks marred the perfection of his body, though. In her eyes, they were testaments of his strength and only added to the attraction she already felt.

She'd known that she wanted him from the minute she saw him again after the past few years. But now, he was flesh and blood and heading toward her.

He had felt her eyes on him but was pleased and shocked by her open admiration. His lips turned up a bit, but he suppressed the smile, fearing it would appear too cocky to her. Still, he was secretly thrilled to have finally caught Emma's eye. And her heart. He thought it was only fair since she'd had his eye and his heart for so long. And had been the subject of every wet dream he'd had since he was fifteen. Every time he thought she was out of his head, she crept back in around two a.m. to stake her claim. He leaned on the fence, removed his hat, wiped his brow and replaced the hat.

"The animals are magnificent," she finally said, not taking her gaze from his chest.

The smile escaped his lips this time at her slight blush. This was a far cry from the woman who had tempted him on the stage and then turned to mush over the thought of coming back home. And her ever-changing persona fascinated him. "Yes they are," he felt his throat go dry. She was magnificent.

As sexy as Harley had been in both her business suit and her g-string, she didn't hold a candle to Emma in her faded jeans and white tank top. He jumped over the fence to close the distance between them. His eyes were focused on her lips and when she ran her pink tongue across them, it took every ounce of strength he had to not grab her and claim her mouth.

"How long have you been breaking wild horses?" she asked, still staring blatantly at his chest. He smiled and returned the favor.

"All my life," he leaned against the fence to keep a healthy distance between them. "But you wouldn't know that, would you?"

"I suppose not. It's very physical."

He watched her tongue dart out again to wet her lips. Dry lips. The sign of a woman in desperate need of a kiss. What had Rhett said to Scarlett? She needed to be kissed. And often. And by someone who knew how. Thank you, Julie Wilson, senior year girlfriend. Because of her, he could recognize the Scarlett in Emma. "Very," he agreed.

"And dangerous?"

"Yes," the husky tone in his voice surprised him. She was under his skin.

"They're beautiful," she was trying to focus on the two Mustangs in the corral, but Shane knew he had her complete attention.

"Yeah," he took a step toward her and watched her back straighten. "Beautiful, exotic, breathtaking." But the third word, only inches separated them. She neither spoke nor flinched. But damn her, she licked her lips. That tongue was going to be his undoing.

"Wh-what is your favorite part?"

"Uncovering their secrets," his voice was still laced with desire. "Sometimes the wild ones have a gentle side, and sometimes the shy ones house a hellcat. And sometimes you get both."

He wasn't talking about horses. His eyes had narrowed to a serious expression. Even the shadow cast by his Stetson couldn't hide the indication. And Emma was defenseless. She turned toward the horses, breaking the magnetic pull his body seemed to have on hers. "And what do you have here?"

He turned also so that when he spoke, his breath made the tiny hairs on her neck stand up. "Both," the word was barely a whisper. It sent a shiver down her spine.

"Lunch," he said finally. "I think it's time for lunch."

"I'm cooking," she offered.

He laughed. Her disasters in Home Ec had been legendary. "You?" he teased.

"I can boil noodles," she retorted, punching his arm and then wishing she hadn't been so bold as to touch him. Even the impact of her fist on his biceps sent warmth throughout her body.

"For ..." he was not unaffected by her touch, but he was drawn in by the playful look in her eyes.

"Spaghetti." She watched his smile widen and spread to his eyes.

"It's too hot for spaghetti," he offered.

"It's never too hot for a little Italian," she winked. She felt his eyes on her back as she walked back toward the house. She couldn't help the smile that crossed her lips.

* * * *

"Is cowboy music all you've got?" Emma yelled across the living room.

"I live on a ranch and break horses. What do you think?" he was still partially wet from his shower and was clad only in a pair of Levi's as he walked back into the room.

"Well, there's no accounting for taste," she licked her bottom lip, probably unconsciously, but it was enough to send heat straight to his groin.

"Try this," he moved to stand beside her and rummage through the CD collection. "Ah, here it is," he handed her one of many CDs that had been left behind when a former girlfriend had hit the road. He smiled. She'd been in such a hurry to leave, she'd left half of her clothes and most of her music.

"Totally 80's?" she raised an eyebrow, taking the CD from his hand.

"Yeah, I think there's some of your old cheerleader music on there. I'm sure you remember a routine or two." He knew he certainly did. In fact, he could still run through most of the routines in his head without having to concentrate. Of course, in his head, she was not wearing the cute cheerleader costume …

"You're so funny. I lasted a good, what, month as a cheerleader?" she smiled and placed the CD in the player. "Now go away while I cook."

"You're not gonna order out while my head is turned, are you?" He couldn't resist taking a jab at her.

She swiped away the finger that he had wagged in her face. "I learned very few things in the past couple of years. How to cook was one of them. Now go." She shooed him out with her hands.

"Yes, ma'am. I'll be on the porch with a beer. Call me when it's ready."

Shane pulled the ring out of his pocket. It had been burning a hole there all weekend. He hadn't gotten rid of it, even though he bought it long before he found Emma again with the intention of finding her and giving it to her one day.

"It's ready," Emma stepped out onto the porch. He shoved it back into his pocket. But when he turned to look at her, he knew he wanted to do it right now.

"Come here," he said, a lazy, devious grin on his face.

"What?" her smile was hesitant.

He pulled her onto his lap. "You know I'm not too good with words."

"You do fine," she teased.

"Well, you might not think so when I'm done."

"Okay," she eyed him warily.

"I want you to know that I love you. I love having you here. And I want you to stay."

"I am staying. And I love you, too." She reached up to kiss him, but he stopped her, placing a finger on her lips.

"No. I want you to stay forever. I want you to marry me." He shifted, pulled the ring from his pocket. "And if you do, you get a prize."

Emma's face lit up at the sight of the ring. It wasn't a diamond. It was a sapphire. Something, in his opinion, that would always remind him of the Louisiana sky and of how much he loved her.

"So?"

"I can't." She dragged herself from his lap.

"What do you mean, you can't?"

"I can't stay here with you. I can't marry you."

"What are you afraid of? Your past? Damn it, Emma, you have to let it go."

"I can't let it go. Do you know what it's like to have put so many people in danger? Do you know how it feels to know that monster touched me? That I let him into my life? Into their lives?"

"I couldn't stop him any more than you could, and I was a cop then."

"Well, I was his wife."

"And not his keeper."

She leaned on the porch railing, her back to him, her shoulders slumped. "I should have been able to stop him."

"No one could have." He placed his hands on her

shoulders, wishing he could take away her pain, knowing there was nothing he could do to save her if his love wasn't enough.

"Could you take me home? Take me back to Baton Rouge. I need to forget about this place." She turned to face him, tears streaking down her face.

"About me?"

"About everything."

"Then I'm going to stay with you. I'll move in with you."

"I didn't ask you to. I need to go back. I need to be Harley again."

"No. I won't let you go back to that world. You were hiding out there. You need to face the past."

"I can't. I'm not strong enough."

"But I am." He pulled her against him, trying to quell the pain in his chest when she tried to push away.

"How could you love me?"

"I have always loved you. Nobody holds your past against you. Not me. Not your family. Not this town." Stroking her hair, he placed tiny kisses on the top of her head.

"What can I do to let go of the pain?"

"I have a few suggestions. I'm pretty resourceful, you know."

"And?"

"Therapy for one."

"No," she started shaking her head, "I've been there already. No help."

"The other suggestion is that you volunteer in town. Work with kids who need your help, kids whose pain is like yours. People who feel as if everyone is looking at them, judging them."

"I don't think I could ..."

"You could. I'm with you. I'll help you."

"So you've thought this through."

"I bought this ring a long time ago with the intention of putting it on your finger. I'm not going to rest until you wear it, so, yes, I have thought it all through."

A slight smile spread across her lips. "You are something else."

"That's what they tell me."

"I don't know if you realize what you're getting in to."

"I know exactly what I'm getting in to. Now, will you marry me?"

She wiped the tears from her eyes and nodded slowly. "Yes, Shane. I'll marry you."

Epilogue

"We've got to stop meeting like this." Shane smiled at Emma. In the past few months, it seemed like they had danced more than should be humanly possible. Tonight was no exception. Again were they on a make shift dance floor encircled with white lights and pink balloons.

"What, you're tired of dancing with me already?" she teased.

"Never. I'm just tired of getting all dressed up to dance with you. There's a lot to be said for jeans."

"But you look so handsome in your black suit. Even if you insisted on wearing the cowboy hat," she rolled her eyes.

"You love this hat," he challenged. "Besides, the stripper last night thought it was quite attractive."

"I see. And what else did she have to say?"

"Nothing much." He grinned. "I asked her to marry me today."

"Oh?" she raised an eyebrow.

"Yeah. She turned me down flat. Said she was marrying some cowboy loser. He got her knocked up so she's gotta quit dancing."

She punched him lightly. "Lucky for me, I guess."

"Damn lucky."

"So, did she dance for you in the champagne room?"

"No. She came home with me instead. Said she'd be mine for the night, but promised to hang up her g-string after the night was done." He planted a kiss on the tip of her nose. "And I told her she sure as hell better."

"I never was very good at it anyway," she shrugged.

"Baby, you were the best I've ever seen."

"You're just saying that because I agreed to marry you."

"No, I'm saying that because you're the only woman who has ever stirred my blood like that."

She rested her head on his shoulder. This was home. "Shane?"

"Yeah?"

"How long do you think we have to dance like this before they'll let us leave?"

"You know you have to throw the bouquet first. And, please," he laughed, "don't hit your sister with it."

She joined him in the laughter, "I wouldn't dream of it."

The End

Blood Feud

By

Kimberly Zant

New to town, I'd used up a tank of gas pounding the pavement in search of a place to light before I had to spend all of my savings on a hotel. I tried to be philosophical about the situation. I'd be living here now. I needed to learn my way around, but moving wasn't cheep and I was going to have to count my pennies until I was fully settled, so it was hard to be completely off hand about it.

There'd been a few frustrations in the exercise, like getting lost more times than I liked to count, but I'd found a place that suited both my budget and my temperament. I was trying to decide what furniture I needed and where to put the pieces I'd brought with me when I'd discovered the view from my apartment was a beautiful one--not the scenery, the local wildlife.

My living room window looked right down into the walled yard of the neighbor's house--sort of--meaning I could see into it--and from a distance at least, the man next door was enough to send any red blooded woman's libido into overdrive.

Impossible as it seemed, he looked even better close up, because I'd nearly broke my neck to get back downstairs to unload the car so that I could get a better look at the young god sprawled half naked in a lawn chair next door.

Disappointment filled me when I reached the parking lot. The wall was just a tad too high for me to look over it casually. I suppose that was why I hadn't noticed him to begin with.

I glared at the wall irritably. Climbing on the top of my car and leering at him wasn't what I'd had in mind. He was built like a young god, but that didn't mean he looked like one. For all I knew the body was just a fluke and the face that went with it a total turnoff.

I was still trying to figure out how I was going to get a better look at him when I slammed the trunk lid, hoisted the box I'd removed from the trunk on one hip and started back. There was a face peering at me from the other side of the wall. A jolt went through me, partly because I was stunned to discover he'd come to check me out without any pretense of casual curiosity, partly because finding someone staring at me was completely unexpected, and partly because if this face went with the body I'd seen from my window it was hard to fathom why there wasn't also a harem of women draped all over him.

Blinking rapidly, as if someone had just swung a punch at me, I braked as abruptly as if I'd run into the wall he was leaning on.

His dark gaze scanned me from the top of my head right down to my sandals without any attempt to hide his carnal interest. His gaze was heated when his eyes met mine again and so was I. One corner of a devilishly kissable mouth tipped upward, displaying an equally devilish dimple. The smile kept growing, his lips parting slowly to reveal a set of teeth that looked amazingly white next to his dark olive skin. "Movin' in, chère?"

Feeling as giddy and awkward as a teenager, I merely gaped at him, my mind struggling to decipher the unfamiliar accent. "Uh--yes," I finally managed a little weakly.

"You doan sound too sure, chère. I didn't scare you, did I? 'Cause that wasn't what I had in mind. I just figured I might as well introduce myself an' offer you a hand, seein' as how we're gonna be neighbors."

I managed a tremulous smile. "That's so sweet of you to offer, but I've only got a few things with me. Most of my stuff is in storage. I thought I'd look around for someone to move it for me tomorrow."

"Hold on."

I blinked in surprise and stepped back as he hoisted himself up on top of the wall. Every muscle in both arms and his chest and belly strained and rippled as he straightened his arms, supporting his body momentarily, and then flung one leg over the top.

Every muscle in my body clenched, especially those in my lower belly, as I stared in opened mouthed wonder at all those rippling muscles. I hadn't even known men had that many muscles in their bodies.

"Beau," he murmured with a wide smile as he landed beside me.

I was so busy staring at the happy trail that led from his belly button to Godzilla, faithfully cupped by his snug jeans, that it took me several moments to gather my wits. "I'm … uh …Jillian," I supplied after a frantic scramble around my mind in search of my identity. "Beau?"

He grimaced, rubbing the dark shadow of beard along his jaw. "Short for Beauregard. DuMauier."

My face flamed. I prodded my mind for the little bit of French I remembered from high school. Beautiful view? I knew that was close to the mark if not the exact translation. I'd thought it was a nickname, but if anybody deserved to wear such a name, this man certainly did.

"Oh!" I said. Thoroughly rattled by now, I stuck my hand out. "Jillian."

The easy grin and the dimple appeared again, this time accompanied by a husky chuckle that made my kegels clench like they had something to hang on to-- or wanted something to place a stranglehold on--which they definitely did. "I did rattle you just a tad, din I, chère?"

I went back to blinking, wondering how he could tell. "Cook," I added hastily, realizing that I'd already given him my first name twice and feeling my face heat up and flash like a neon sign.

"On occasion," he responded. "Especially for purty ladies."

I began to have the bizarre feeling that I'd stepped into a different world and the natives didn't speak my language. It dawned on me after a moment, though, that he'd thought my name was a question. "Uh … I meant, my last name. It's Cook."

He chuckled again, his face darkening just enough to thoroughly captivate me, as if I hadn't been to start with. "Now I'm disappointed. Here I thought we had somethin' goin'."

I wasn't shy ordinarily, but I wasn't exactly bold either. I burned to say something ribald, though. Dinner and a fuck? "We could," I stammered. "I mean, I could … cook." My wits were scrambled! "Uh … actually, I don't have any of the kitchen stuff yet."

"So--maybe I should invite you to my place instead? I cook a mean steak."

I wanted to accept, desperately, which was the main reason I thought it unwise. "I'd like that," I managed to say politely. "But I guess I should get settled in before I consider … uh …." I floundered, trying to decide whether the invitation constituted a date, or if it was just a neighborly sort of 'housewarming' thing. I didn't want to sound as if I assumed he was interested in me that way when I'd barely met him. "…Playing" Eekk! Where the fuck had that come from? "Work before …uh … play, you know." God! Kill me now! That was unbelievably stupid! "Because I'm not settled in and couldn't return the invitation."

I could tell from his expression that he was trying to decide if I'd lost my keeper or had way too much to drink.

This was really going badly!

I rubbed my temple absently, wondering if I'd gotten sun stroke, or if it was just my libido that had fried my brain. "I'm sorry. I'm just really tired," I said on inspiration. "Long drive, and all the packing before, sleeping in a strange place. I'm really not a moron. Honestly."

He gave me a look of sympathy. "Tell ya what, baby. I jus' happen to have access to a truck and some men with strong arms and backs. Why don't I give you a hand with the movin'?"

"That is so sweet!" I exclaimed, totally surprised to discover that he was as nice as he was beautiful. "I wouldn't want to impose, though."

He took the box from me and guided me toward the apartment house. "I consider it an investment."

I looked at him in surprise, wondering if I was going to get to pay him back in trade. Oh what a job that would be! "An investment?"

"I'll get you moved in, and you cook dinner for me."

* * * *

Blinded by my hair, I felt my way to the door the following morning in answer to a persistent summons I'd tried to ignore and discovered I couldn't. Discovering Beau on the other side of the door looking like every woman's wet dream was like getting a bucket of ice water in the face. My sleep deprived brain kicked into overdrive, filling my mind with an image of me standing at the door looking, I felt certain, like the wrath of god.

"Ready?" he asked cheerfully.

My brain went into Neanderthal mode then--bed--sleep--ready? Wait, I wasn't in bed and he was outside of my apartment. Something didn't click. "For what?" I asked cautiously.

"I tol' you I'd bring some guys to help move you in, remember?"

I shoved a hand into the lock of hair hanging over my face and pushed it back. "It's tomorrow? I mean, day, already?"

He chuckled, propping his shoulder against the doorframe. "I can come back later, chère, but I cain't guarantee these guys gonna be sober. It's Saturday, and that means party time, especially since I promised them a case of beer a piece to help out. They're gonna be into it if we don't get down stairs."

I did not want to start moving this early in the day! However, beggars couldn't be choosers and I knew if I turned him away I was going to have to look for help on Monday. "Can you give me a couple of minutes to change? Dress?" I added when I discovered I was standing in the doorway in my oversized t-shirt and panties.

He looked me over with interest. "I'll wait in the truck."

I should have asked him in, I supposed. There was just enough of a questioning lilt at the end to clue me that he was fishing for an invitation to come in. Instead, I smiled, promised to hurry, and shut the door in his face. Dashing into the bathroom, I raced around frantically trying to do everything at once. I'm not certain it was a fruitful exercise in the sense that it helped me get ready faster, but it got the blood pumping in my veins and heightened alertness.

I wanted, desperately, to primp, but this wasn't a date, be he ever so handsome, and I didn't want to be too obvious. Compromising, I took a moment to throw some eyeliner and mascara on, combed my hair, jumped into a pair of worn jeans and an equally worn t-shirt and dashed out the door.

There was a monster truck parked at the curb. Leaning casually against one big fender, was Beau, his arms crossed over his chest.

On the front door was a magnetic sign that read: Beauregard Construction.

At the time, it didn't actually strike me as odd that he'd used his first name in naming his company, but then I still wasn't at tiptop mental acuity either. I discovered when he'd walked me around and helped me get in by placing a hand under my ass that the truck had a backseat, which was filled with men.

Uttering a gasp at that well placed hand, I shot upwards into the cab and landed with a bounce. Grinning like a Cheshire cat, Beau closed the door and made the trip back to his own door. He slid me a provocative glance as he settled behind the wheel, leaving me in no doubt that the hand incident hadn't been accidental.

I gave him a look.

"This is part of my crew--Etienne, Bobby Joe, and Clarence."

I turned to smile at them in acknowledgement of the introduction. "I'm Jillian. I really appreciate you guys coming to help out on your day off."

They politely assured me they were happy to do it and, feeling a little more relaxed, I turned to fasten my belt as Beau started the truck, giving him directions to the storage facility.

He took a detour through Mac's and bought everyone breakfast and coffee, ignoring my protests that I could pay for my own.

I couldn't help but notice none of the guys protested. Nibbling my food, I began to make a mental tally of what the Beau was paying his 'volunteers' to help me move and decided that it was actually fair compensation for what probably wasn't going to take more than half a day. It was comforting in one way--I didn't have to feel deeply obligated to them for their help beyond the fact that they'd given up part of a day off doing something I was sure they didn't particularly want to do.

With Beau, it was another situation entirely. I could see if he had his way I was going to be indebted big time and this was either going to translate into several cooked meals, or ....

I was surprised to discover I had mixed feelings about the possibility. It occurred to me after a few moments, though, that I had no problem with the guy's animal sex appeal, at least not insofar as my drive went. The problem was I knew I couldn't be the only gal in town panting after him.

He was my neighbor. Bad, bad idea! Because if we had a go and it flopped, it was going to be hard to avoid each other. And if he had one of those revolving front doors, it might irritate me to watch the traffic jam.

So what was wrong with a little casual sex, I asked myself irritably? I hadn't known the guy two days. I wasn't looking desperately for some sort of commitment because I felt a burning need for the old husband, kids, and white picket fence. It wasn't as if I was one of those people that went around falling in love all the time. I'd never been more than mildly fond of any of the guys I'd dated before. I could handle it.

Maybe.

Within an hour and a half of arriving at the storage facility, the men had pretty much everything I owned loaded up on the back and were looking for any spaces where they might wedge in the last few boxes.

"What sort of construction do you guys do?" I asked curiously when we'd climbed into the truck again, fairly impressed by the fact that there hadn't been a great deal of huffing and groaning going on while they were loading.

"Carpentry," Beau said almost in unison with the guys in back. "My crew's the fastest in the city. We can frame up an entire house in a week, have it dried in in two."

I wasn't completely ignorant of the trade, but I wasn't familiar enough either to know if that was as impressive as it sounded like to me or if they were trying to pull one over on me. "Y'all can build a whole house in two weeks?"

Beau grinned. "A small house, no more than 1500 square feet. Framed up and dried in. That's exterior doors, windows, roof, and moisture barrier. That's not turn key."

"Oh." I thought that over. "What's turn key?"

They all chuckled over that one. "Ready to walk in and settle."

"Y'all build a lot of houses?" I asked, turning in my seat to include the gang in the back.

One of the guys, Bobby Joe, I thought, shot a glance at Beau. "We're working on a housing subdivision right now. Twenty units contracted, maybe more if we get them done as promised. We got half."

When I glanced at Beau, I saw he wasn't looking exactly pleased. I wasn't certain of what had brought on that somber look, but decided to drop the subject since it was obvious there was something about it that was bugging him.

Despite my attempt to change the subject, the mood seemed to have swung to a far less cheerful one and I was glad when we got back to the apartment house. Evidently, in spite of Beau's bragging on his crew, there were problems with the job.

Either that or the fact that he'd only gotten half the units was a sore point for him.

Oddly enough since I hadn't known him long at all, it almost seemed out of character that he would be so competitive about the job. He'd seemed so laid back about pretty much everything else I hadn't pictured him as an aggressive business man.

The man had depth.

I longed to plum them.

And it was one of my worst ideas, I was sure.

I owed him a dinner, though.

It took a bit longer to haul everything up the stairs and into the apartment than it had to empty the storage facility, but it was only a little after noon when they lugged the last of it up the stairs, set it in my apartment and beat a retreat almost before I'd realized they were gone. Shrugging, I scrounged up a bite to eat and went to work settling in. Mindful of the 'deal' I'd made with Beau, I started in the kitchen, worked my way through the living room and then pooped out when I got to the bedroom and sprawled across my bed for a nap.

To my disappointment, although I was ready for battle that evening, Beau didn't show. Contrary creature that I was, when he didn't, I went from a vague irritation and uneasiness about being manipulated into an obligation to entertain him to a sense of having been rejected and abandoned.

By the following morning I'd reached a state where I had to fight the temptation to peer out my window to see what the man was up to.

He was either damned good, I reflected irritably, or not nearly as interested as he'd appeared to be.

Since I had pretty much put the place in order and was way too restless to remain cooped up in the apartment, I headed out to fill up my gas tank and buy groceries to fill in the yawning cavity of the virtually empty refrigerator and kitchen cabinets.

* * * *

The man was fine. There was just no getting around it. Wearing nothing but a pair of cut off jeans--and those well worn in all the best places--I could see at a glance that there wasn't nothing on him that wasn't downright scrumptious. My blood commenced to pumping through my veins like warm molasses when he favored me with a laughing glance from those beautiful baby blues of his and a slow smile.

"I ain't seen you around here before," he drawled. "Movin' in, or passin' through?"

"I just moved out from Albany."

His dark blond brows rose. "Yankee country? Chère, don cha know you're in occupied territory?"

"Excuse you!" I said testily. "Albany Georgia."

He chuckled. "Oh! Well, now, that's different. A peach? What brings you to Cajun country?"

The Cajuns, I thought, fanning myself. "I got transferred by the company."

His gaze wandered leisurely down my body and up again. I suppose I might have taken exception if any other man had given me that kind of once over, but there was just something about the hungry way the guy looked at me that made me feel warm all over.

"I'm not even gonna guess what you do. You look like you might pass a mean punch. Name's Beauregard, but my friends call be Beau. What's your name?"

I blinked, rapidly, wondering if half the guys in the county had that name. "Weird! Sorry. I didn't mean that the way it sounded, but I just met a guy named Beauregard--unless he was joking."

His smile vanished. "Ugly son-of-a-bitch with black hair and snake eyes?"

I frowned. That didn't really sound like the guy--at all, because right up until I'd run into this blond hunk I'd thought he was the most gorgeous in the land. "Uh--you must be thinking of somebody else. This guy was around your age, I guess. Tall, black hair, green eyes...."

His lips formed a thin line. "That'd be him."

Frowning, he turned and topped off my gas tank and twisted the cap back on.

I dragged my wallet out and handed him a couple of twenties.

He stared at the money for several moments and his good humor returned. His blue eyes were dancing with laughter when he looked up at me again. "I usually charge a bit more'n that, but for you, chère ...."

Confusion settled over me along with the suspicion that we were on two different wave lengths. "The pump says $28."

He glanced at the pump. "Oh! Well, chère, you probably ought to give that to the gas station attendant. They tend to get a little peeved if they don't get paid for the gas."

"You don't work here?" I asked blankly.

"Nope. I just figured I'd mosey on over and introduce myself."

I felt my face turn red.

"You didn't give me your name," he reminded me as I turned away and looked around for the guy I was supposed to pay, torn between amusement and annoyance.

"No, I didn't," I said without glancing back at him.

"Or your number."

I ignored that.

"I'll wait here."

To my surprise, I discovered when I got back to my car that he was waiting.

"I think we got off to a rocky start, Chère. Name's Beauregard Chevalier, but my closest friends call me Beau."

I didn't know whether to laugh or scream for the cops. "Jillian," I said finally. "Jillian Cook."

"For now."

I lifted my brows at him questioningly.

He shrugged. "Well, if you're gonna be the mother of my children, you're just going to have to take my name. It's a family tradition."

I felt my jaw drop.

Chuckling, he tapped my chin. "You'll catch flies, darlin'. I was just headin' down to the cabin for a fish fry. Wanna come along?"

"I don't even know you!"

"Well, darlin', you ain't gonna get to know me any better sittin' in your apartment all alone--but we could go to your place, if you prefer."

I shouldn't have been tempted. I was, though, and I had a bad feeling he could see it in my eyes. He favored me with another one of those slow grins that set my insides to doing a jitter.

"I'm safe. If you don wanna take my word for it, just ask anybody around the store here. They all know me."

It was unnerving, but I was new in town and didn't know a soul. He had a point. How was I going to change that if I didn't take a chance? I glanced around and spied a young girl just coming out of the store. Before I could ask her if she knew him, the little girl spied him. Her face lit up like a Christmas tree and she scampered over to stand beside us, looking up at him worshipfully. "Uncle Beau! You comin' down to Granma's for the fish fry?"

"Shore thing, little bit. I was just tryin' to convince this purty lady here to come with me."

I was almost more embarrassed by that discovery than I had been nervous about the invitation to start with. "It's a family thing?"

"And friends."

"It's tempting, but …."

"Come on, sugar," he said leaning close enough to whisper in my ear conspiratorially, "you can't just leave me to face this all by my lonesome. Hop in. You can follow me."

* * * *

I'd been around some strange families, but this one was really different. He'd introduced them as brothers, but I had to wonder if it was some sort of joke and I hadn't gotten the punch line. Bobby Lee was part black--handsome in an exotic way with his gray eyes and coffee and cream complexion--Jubal was part Hispanic and Jeb part Asian--All tall, handsome, and well built, but bearing no real family resemblance that I could see. If they were his brothers, they had to be half brothers, but I wondered if they were related at all or just good buddies.

There was something about their names that teased me, too. "Is Jeb short for Jebidiah?" I asked curiously, trailing my fingers along the picket fence as we crossed the yard, heading toward the dock.

He chuckled. "Nah. He's named after Jeb Stuart. Ma's a history buff."

I stopped abruptly, staring at him in the waning light of the late afternoon as the rest of the names clicked in my head and amusement surfaced. "Robert E. Lee, Jeb Stuart, Jubal Early, and Pierre Beauregard."

He grinned. "I see you're a history buff, too."

I shook my head at his teasing smile, wondering how much he said that I could believe and how much was pure bullshit. I was going to have to get me a pair of wading boots if I meant to hang around this guy. The bullshit was getting deep. "Are they really your brothers or were you just teasing me?"

"Ahh, you noticed we don't favor much. Ma's always been a free spirit. We're half brothers--but she's a god fearin' woman. Married every last one of our fathers. I was a near miss myself. But they finished up their 'I dos' before I arrived, and on the good side, the preacher was right there to baptize me when I got here."

"I don't know what to make of you, Beau Chevalier!" I said with a chuckle. "Are you never serious?"

He slipped a hand around my waist, moving closer. Amusement gleamed in his eyes as he looked down at me, but there was something else there, as well. "I was serious as a heart attack about you bein' the mother of my children," he murmured, dipping his head until his lips were hovering just above mine.

"Were you?" I asked, teasing him back, trying to decide whether I wanted him to kiss me or not--not much of a contest really. His mouth had been driving me crazy ever since I'd laid eyes on him. I really, really wanted to see what it could do besides tease verbally. Lifting closer, I brushed my lips along his.

"You don't believe in love at first sight, chère?"

I nipped his chin with the edge of my teeth. I'd had enough teasing. I wanted the serious wooing to commence. "You mean lust," I said, chuckling.

He drew back, studying me. "Now you done gone and hurt my feelings."

He looked dead serious and confusion filled me. "Seriously?" I asked doubtfully.

I caught a flash of a grin a split second before he covered my mouth with his, but it barely registered. His mouth, like his voice, was as hot and sweet as warm honey and it brought me instantly to dew point. My heart began to beat so frantically I couldn't catch my breath. Weakness and dizziness washed through me as I felt the heated, faintly rough caress of his tongue along mine, felt the light skate of his hands as he stroked them along my back and buttocks, drawing me closer until I could feel his hard erection against my belly.

I was disappointed when he withdrew, sucking first my upper lip and then the lower before he drew back to study my face.

"Course we'll need to practice a lot."

My mind was so much mush it took several moments for that to sink in. When it finally did, I popped him playfully on the shoulder. "You are such an ass!"

He chuckled as if I'd paid him a compliment. "I'm serious, sugar. Ma always says 'practice makes perfect' and I'm a firm believer in it."

"I expect you've already had plenty of practice," I said dryly, still amused, but faintly irritated, too, because I'd fallen for the line.

"There's where you're wrong, chère. I been savin' myself for the right woman."

"Right!"

Laughing, he caught me, curling an arm around me and dragging me close again when I pushed away from him and started to stalk back toward the house.

Caging me with his arms looped loosely around my waist, he studied me for several moments and sobered. "I'm more than willin' to take you to my place and prove it, sugar, but you've got to promise me you won't breathe a word to a soul, 'cause nobody else around here knows."

I burst out laughing. "You are completely incorrigible, Beau Chevalier!"

His smiled faded. His arms tightened, drawing me close once more. "Not completely, darlin'. I just haven't had any incentive to reform before."

The man could make love with his mouth like no one I'd ever known. My heart shot from 0 to 60 in two seconds flat, my perception of anything outside of his touch was instantly obliterated, as if someone had injected adrenaline laced with narcotics into me. A cloud of warmth enveloped me, closed around both of us. The air felt charged, every tiny hair follicle on my body lifting and shifting into acute sensitivity.

I didn't know how his leisurely exploration of my mouth with his tongue, or my body with his hands, could produce such a powerful sense of urgency inside of me, but there was no denying that it did. Heated images of our bodies entwined rose in my mind as he stroked his tongue along mine and my sex felt the intimate pleasure as surely as if the turgid flesh against my belly was stroking my passage instead. Feeling weak and heavy, I shifted closer, pressing my aching breasts against his hard chest, moving my mound restlessly against the hard ridge of flesh I wanted inside of me so badly I began to shake with the need. The pressure was just enough to tease me and make me want more, to evoke fresh images in my mind of bare skin against bare skin.

My need communicated itself to him and his slow, savoring touch became more urgent, more demanding. A tremor went through him when I closed my mouth around his tongue and sucked it. His arms tightened and then he slipped one hand down my back to cup my buttocks and bring me hard against his hips.

For several aching moments, he held me tightly and then, as if with a strenuous effort, he relaxed the tight hold, stroked my tongue almost apologetically and withdrew, plucking at my lips before he lifted his head to look down at me. "I should get you home," he said, his voice husky.

My mind instantly leapt to my bed. It took an effort to lift my heavy eyelids, but once I'd managed it slowly filtered into my heated brain that we were standing in his mother's front yard--and it was dark, not so dark that everyone couldn't see us, but dark for me to be out as unfamiliar as I was with the area.

Consternation began to nudge the desire still pounding in my blood aside. I pulled away from him, looking around a little vaguely, trying to gather my scattered wits. "I drove," I said finally, more to remind myself than him.

His mouth curled up on side. "I know. I'll follow you to make sure you get to your place OK."

Thoroughly rattled, I had no desire to have to run the gauntlet of his family on my way out. I knew it was awfully rude, but I had a feeling I looked like I felt, as if I'd just been fucked silly. Evidently he was as anxious to avoid his family as I was. Grasping my arm, he led me back across the yard toward my car, calling his goodbyes to several dark shapes on the front porch of the cabin.

Embarrassed, I waved, too, thanked them for 'inviting' me and climbed into my car with a strong sense of relief trying to remember how I'd gotten to the place.

He held onto the door. "You alright, chère?"

I pasted a vague smile on my lips. "Sure."

"Remember the way back? Or should I lead till we get back to more familiar territory?"

"I'll follow you back to the station," I said, giving up any attempt to try to pretend I had any idea of where I actually was, wondering if he meant to part ways with me there or follow me back to my apartment.

The throbbing need inside of me had dulled to a low roar by the time we got to the station, enough that I was beginning to wonder at the wisdom of showing him where I lived--not enough to actually dredge up any defenses. The moment he assured me he had no intention of allowing me to wander around the city at night without his escort, anticipation began to rev through me again.

He pulled in behind me at my apartment and got out, sending a long, thoughtful glance in the direction of my neighbor's house. I studied him a little uncertainly when I'd gotten out, wondering if he was merely going to see me to my door or waiting for an invitation to take up where we'd left off.

His hesitancy provoked an unaccustomed spurt of carelessness in me. "You coming up?"

He turned and fixed me with an inscrutable gaze and finally ambled toward me, draping an arm over my shoulders. "A gentleman always walks a lady to her door," he murmured against my ear, slipping his arm from my shoulders to my waist as I headed inside. I was as nervous and jittery as a caffeine addict on ten cups of coffee by the time we got to my door. It took me several minutes to find my key. He took it from my shaking hand, pushed it into the lock and pushed the door open.

Still uncertain of whether he meant to merely let me in and leave, I turned as I stepped inside, almost colliding with him as he followed me.

"Would you like some ...?"

I didn't get the rest of the offer of refreshment out. Kicking the door shut behind him, he slipped his arms around me and dragged me close almost in the same moment. His mouth this time was demanding as it descended over mine. The moment his scent and taste and heat spread through me my body instantly bridged the thirty minute or so gap between his last kiss and that moment and I was ready, willing, and eager to the point of desperate need.

Instantly throwing caution and any pretense of coyness to the wind, I slipped my hands beneath his shirt, exploring his skin. Hard muscle and silken flesh met my inquisitive touch, spurring a sharp jolt of pleasure through me that heated my body to dew point even before he took his cue from me and slipped his hands beneath my shirt. Gliding his palms over my back briefly in exploration, he slipped one downward after a moment, holding my hips as he arched against me and then pushed one hand beneath the waist of my jeans to cup one cheek of my ass.

I didn't want to let go of him long enough to discard my clothes, or move away by so much as a hair's breadth, but the need to feel his bare skin against mine was nearly overwhelming. My breasts were full and achingly sensitive. I pressed more tightly against him as he made love to my mouth with his tongue, demanding the fulfillment my body had begun to crave, imagining the silken glide of his cock along my passage.

When his hands moved around my waistband and fumbled with the snap of my jeans, I pulled away. He looked at me inquiringly, his breathing nearly as ragged as mine, but he did not try to pull me back. Grasping his hand, I led him to my room wordlessly.

He pulled me close again once we were inside the room, but I'd had enough teasing. I wanted to see the beautiful package I'd been imagining ever since I'd first seen him. Pushing away from him after only a brief kiss, I peeled my shirt off and tossed it aside, kicked my sandals off and shimmied out of my jeans and panties.

A slow, seductive strip tease might have been better, but I was in no mood to wait. Naked, I climbed onto the bed and rolled onto my side to watch him undress.

He dragged his t-shirt off and tossed it to the floor with mine, nudging his shoes off. Some doubt seemed to shake him, though, as he unfastened his jeans. Instead of shucking them as I had, he merely unzipped them, placed a knee on the mattress beside me and moved over me, settling most of his weight on one arm.

Shy, I wondered? Worried about how he stacked up?

The bashfulness in a guy that had displayed nothing but supreme self confidence right up until that moment not only fascinated me, it sent a flurry of questions through my mind.

I forgot them the moment he nuzzled his way down my throat and took one of my nipples into his mouth, taking a hard drag at the almost painfully engorged flesh that sent a shower of jolting, sizzling desire through me. Threading my fingers through his hair, I sucked in a hard gasp of air and held it as wildfire spread through me, arching up to meet his teasing exploration. A wall of darkness descended over my mind, reminding me of the need to breathe. I managed to drag in another desperate gulp of air as he finally released that nipple and moved to its twin. Thoroughly caught up in the fever of need by the time he ceased to tease my nipples and moved up to capture my lips again, I wrapped one leg around his waist, slipping one hand down until I could grasp his buttocks and then arching against him demandingly.

I could scarcely catch a decent breath of air and broke the kiss, catching his earlobe between my teeth as I released his buttock and tried to wedge my hand between us to cup his cock.

He deftly eluded my attempt, arching against my thigh almost bruisingly.

"Now!" I demanded in a hoarse whisper I hardly recognized as my own.

"Easy, baby," he murmured, nuzzling his face against my neck. "We've got all night."

We could go slow--later--maybe. I was too frantic to feel him inside of me right then to want to wait. Grasping the hand exploring my waist, I guided it downward, over my belly. His thick fingers parted the flesh of my sex, sending new jolts of desire through me that were so intense I gritted my teeth against the nearly unbearable sensations rocking me. I was ready. I was more than ready. If he didn't enter me soon I was going to leave him behind and I didn't want to waste my climax on wishes when there was a perfectly good cock ready and waiting to fill me. "I'm ready now," I said almost petulantly, mindlessly arching against his hand as he teased me with his fingers.

He slipped his hips between my legs and I tensed in hopeful expectation as he pushed his shorts down his hips, fumbling between us with something. A condom appeared in his hand. Ripping the wrapper with his teeth, he lifted away slightly and looked down as he struggled to put it on with one hand.

A mixture of relief and anticipation went through me. I stroked his body, everywhere I could reach, reached down to try to help, and shifted restlessly when I discovered I couldn't reach his cock. Thwarted, mildly disappointed that I hadn't gotten the chance to familiarize myself with his turgid flesh, I contented myself with nuzzling his face and neck and ear, with stroking my hands over the hard flesh I could reach.

Growing impatient with the delay, I explored his ear with my tongue, sucked on the lobe. A shudder went through him. He lifted his head, studied me for a long moment and settled his chest against mine, slipping his arms beneath my shoulders and reacquainting himself with my breasts, my throat. I arched against him, kneading his belly with my mound.

It was enough of an invitation. Breaking off, he grasped one of my thighs, tugged until I bent my knee and then lifted away slightly to match his body to mine. Dizzy, my eyes half closed with the need burning inside me, I looked down to watch. My eyes widened as he pushed the head of his cock against my opening.

I'd likened that beast to Godzilla when I'd seen the bulge in his jeans, but it had been soft then. Rock hard now, it looked like a bludgeon. I gasped, tensed as doubt flooded my mind. He didn't give me the chance to wonder if I could handle that much meat, pushing against me with slow, determined deliberation until my muscles yielded and reluctantly allowed him to enter me. Feeling rather as if I'd just been impaled on a fence post, I squirmed, uncertain suddenly of whether I actually wanted to proceed.

He stopped. Tremors ran through him as he sought my mouth. I wasn't certain whether I wanted him to kiss me into mindlessness again either, but I was helpless against the heated tide that broke over me as he explored my mouth again. Teased already to the crest of release, it took no more than the heat of his mouth and the caress of his tongue to drive me completely beyond reason. Instead of trying to push him away, I arched my hips in a desperate attempt to engulf him.

Uttering a groan, his hips jerked and he drove deeper inside of me. I squirmed harder, fought my own body's resistance to his penetration. My muscles clenched around him. Heat and moisture flooded my passage so that when he thrust again, he embedded himself fully. He dragged his mouth from mine, burrowing his face against my neck. "Don't move," he whispered hoarsely, grinding his teeth, panting for breath, sweat breaking from his pores as he fought to hold onto his control. "I can't hold it, chère. You're so tight, baby. You feel so good."

Tight, I thought a little wildly? A horse would feel tight with that monster. My throat closed as a hard wash of need went through me. I felt my body begin to quake with release and he'd done no more than fill me with his flesh. Uttering a groan as it swept over me, I bucked against him, demanding he move. It pushed him over the edge. Dragging in a ragged breath he began to pump into me in short, deep strokes that had me groaning as if I was dying as wave after wave of rapture thundered through me. I was already coming down when I felt him begin to convulse with his own release. I wrapped my arms and legs tightly around him as he shuttered and quaked and finally went limp and heavy against me.

Panting for breath, I clung to him weakly as long as I could and finally wilted limply to the bed, splayed beneath him, my mind a void in the aftermath of the explosive climax that had pounded through me.

He stirred after many moments had passed, lifted his head to study my face as if he was wondering if I was dead. I managed to lift one eyelid to look back at him as he rolled to one side, carrying me with him. Utterly content, I allowed my mind to wander through the haze of bliss while he stroked me almost apologetically. "It was good for you?" he murmured after a moment.

He had doubts? Apparently he wasn't sure whether that was ecstasy or pain that had had me screaming and thrashing wildly beneath him.

And well he might, I thought, managing a twinge of indignation, realizing why he hadn't let me see before hand the mountain he was expecting me to climb.

Shy? Ha! He'd only been afraid I'd take one look at that thing and run.

I might have, at that.

"Mmm," I murmured nonspecifically.

I was disappointed when he pulled out at last and disposed of the condom, lying limply as he'd left me, as boneless as a jellyfish. He moved over me again, nuzzling me, nipping lightly at my skin.

"That was a dirty trick," I murmured chastisingly, softening the criticism by stroking his back.

"What?" he murmured against my skin.

I could feel his mouth curling, though.

Reaching down, I pinched his ass. "You know exactly what I'm talking about."

He lifted away enough to look down at me. His expression was somber. "I didn't hurt you, chère?"

It took an effort to lift my hand to his cheek. I stroked it, enjoying the faint roughness of his whiskers. I liked his face. I liked everything about the guy. I knew in that moment that I was in deep shit. No way was I going to be able to play with this fire and come out of it unscathed. "Aside from dislocating my hip joints and shoving my womb up to my ribcage, no," I murmured jokingly, lifting up to nibble at his lips. "Let's try that again. I'll try to go easy on you this time."

* * * *

A husky voice speaking in a language I could not decipher invaded my dreams. For several moments I drifted, an image forming in my mind of myself entwined around a beautiful male body while he murmured love words to me in French.

"A fine morning, eh DuMauier? You should hurry, mon ami. I will have the roof on my house before noon and leave you behind."

The voice was louder that time and pierced the mists of sleep. Groggily, I pushed myself up on one elbow and looked around my room vacantly for the source. Beau was standing at my bedroom window, naked, his palms braced against the sill as he stared down at something, or someone, beyond my view.

I collapsed back against the mattress, wondering if I'd moved on to a really weird dream. Apparently the sound distracted him. He ceased taunting whoever it was he'd been annoying and crossed to the bed. The mattress dipped. A moment later I felt him settle on top of me. "I'm sorry, Chère," he murmured, nuzzling his face between my breasts. "Did I wake you?"

Instead of making the obvious retort, I opened one eye a crack. "What timezit?"

He lifted up and looked around until he discovered my clock. "Six."

I closed my eye again. "Morning or night?"

He chuckled and went back to nuzzling me, working his way up from the valley to the peak of one breast and sucking it into his mouth. Blood surged into my nipples as if he'd summoned it with the tug of his mouth. Warmth instantly budded in my belly. I groaned, a sound that was part complaint and part encouragement. "What day is it?"

"Monday."

My eyes flew open. I would've bolted upright except for the fact that he was planted firmly on top of me. "You're not serious?"

"I am always serious with you, chère."

I groaned again, but this time it was less passionate and far more frustrated. "It's my first day. I have to get ready. Oh god! I don't feel like I got any sleep. I'm going to be a zombie at work."

He ignored my attempts to roll him off for several moments, but finally complied, watching me with hungry eyes as I struggled off the bed. One step was all it took to assure me he'd screwed me bowlegged the night before. My inner thighs screamed with pain, small wonder considering he'd played 'make a wish' half the night and my thighs weren't hinged in the middle. I gasped, stopped dead in my tracks, rubbing my abused flesh.

"Poor, my baby," he murmured, laughter in his voice. "Come back to bed. I'll kiss it better."

"Ass," I said without heat. "Any more of that and I'll be crippled for sure."

Ignoring him, I hobbled to the bathroom with as much dignity as I could muster locking the door firmly behind me in case he got any ideas. A lengthy hot shower went a long way toward easing the aches and raising the dead, but I still felt like shit warmed over when I got out. I decided after one look in the mirror that I looked it, too. I looked like I'd been in a brawl and had taken a couple of hits to the eyes.

It was going to take industrial strength makeup to even begin to hide the 'afterglow' of my night.

To my surprise, Beau was waiting for me when I came out. I'd expected him to be long gone. In fact, I was surprised, now that I thought about it, that he'd spent the whole night. Guys like Beau were usually hit and run drivers, pun intended, pouncing on unsuspecting females enthralled by their charms, pounding the hell out of them and then sneaking out before 'the morning after' confrontation.

He grabbed me as I stepped out the door, ripping my towel off and feeling me up thoroughly while he kissed me just as thoroughly. I was weak all over by the time he pulled away, steadied me with a firm grip on my shoulders and gave me one of those slow smiles that made my kegels clench. "See you tonight, chère?"

I smiled at him dreamily.

He popped my bare ass and strode out of the room before I could gather my wits about me. I heard him thundering down the stairs at a gallop. My neighbors were going to hate me, I knew, if he made a habit of that this early in the morning.

Thinking of my neighbors, sent me to the window to peer out.

Beau had just reached his truck. He looked up as he got in, spied me at the window and threw me a wave.

It wasn't until he'd backed out of the drive that it clicked in my mind that he had a magnetic sign on the side of his truck that looked a lot like the neighbor's--

in fact, just like the neighbors. Beauregard Construction.

No way was that just some kind of weird coincidence, I realized, feeling uneasy for no reason that I could fathom at the moment--mostly because my brain was still functioning at one quarter speed. I mulled over it while I dressed and then headed to the kitchen to find sustenance.

The puzzle pieces I'd been trying to fit together seemed to click in place when I was about halfway through my coffee.

I hadn't dreamed Beau had been standing at my window calling down to somebody outside. He had been. DuMauier, and Beau DuMauier had been pissed off when one of his crew mentioned the contract on the houses they were building.

These two lunatics were using the same name for their companies, rival construction companies and I'd just planted my dumb ass squarely in the middle of a feud between two hot blooded and probably hot tempered Cajuns!

* * * *

I was career oriented, and probably a workaholic, but I don't think I'd ever actually dreaded going home after work. I tried telling myself I was just being ridiculous. Even if I had stumbled into the middle of some kind of blood feud, it didn't necessarily follow that I needed to be worried about it. I wasn't actually involved with either one of the guys. The night before had been wild, and I had enjoyed myself like never before, but guys like the Beaus were players. They were just too damned gorgeous to confine themselves to one woman. They probably made a habit of nailing any female that looked in their direction and got snagged by the beautiful package.

Prime example, Beau Chevalier had put on his condom one handed--alright he'd used two to get it started, but mostly with one hand. Most guys needed two hands, both feet, and their teeth to get the damned things on. I'd been with guys that had to have my help and we were both in a sweat of frustration before we managed it.

That had taken practice, a lot of practice--be he ever so humble about being a virgin! Ha! Of course one of the reasons he might have acquired that little knack might have been due to survival from blue balls, because I was willing to bet I hadn't been the first female intimidated by the size of the guy. Case in point--He'd kept me from actually seeing it until it was too late to back out. There'd probably been more than one or two that had taken a look at Godzilla and put their clothes back on.

Looking at it that way, it occurred to me that he might have had a lot more practice getting ready than actually using the thing, but that was hardly the point. One good fuck did not a match make! It was flattering that he'd mentioned an encore, but that didn't mean he'd show.

It was going to be fireworks, though, if he did, and Beau DuMauier decided to collect on his dinner.

Mentally kicking myself, I finally accepted that I had to go home and face the music. I couldn't just abandon my apartment and head for the hills, however tempting the thought was. Clearing my desk, I collected my purse and headed out.

Both trucks were parked in front of the apartment building, nose to nose, when I reached the apartment. Instinct kicked in. Stomping on the gas pedal, I shot past them, glancing in the rear view mirror as I reached the corner to see if I could tell if they'd spotted me. I couldn't be certain. Beau the blond was sitting in the driver's seat, staring at Beau of the black hair, who appeared to be staring back at him but might have been watching my tail pipe as I took the corner and sped off.

I drove two blocks down before I convinced myself I was behaving like a skittish teenager who'd made two dates for the same night because she didn't want to take the chance that she'd be staying home.

Whatever their problem was, it was their problem, not mine.

Unfortunately, by the time I arrived at that conclusion embarrassment was starting to set in big time and as I made two more turns to head back, the cringe factor grew exponentially larger the closer I got to my destination. Irritation for my predicament set in behind that, but I decided I could blame that on them--and capricious fate. I hadn't chosen to move in beside one and then meet the other at the gas station. Fate was working against me.

Both men were out of their trucks when I turned into the drive, but they were so busy bristling at each other like two cur dogs who'd both decided to take a piss on the same fire hydrant they hardly noticed me.

I debated whether to approach them or not when I'd parked the car and gotten out. I couldn't make out what they were saying to each other--either because their accents were so thick and unfamiliar or because they were actually speaking to each other in French, but I could see 'good old boy' all over them. The stance was tense, waiting for that sucker punch. They were both smiling, the feral sort of smile southern boys always got on their faces while they were thinking up subtle and not so subtle insults and preparing to beat the shit out of the guy they were smiling at.

Beau Chevalier, I noticed, was oh-so-casually paring his nails with a pocket knife.

Beau DuMauier was playing doctor with his, digging a splinter out of his hand--or not. Either way, it was nothing more than a pretense. When the knives came out, the discussion was serious.

That cinched it for me. I headed into the apartment house and up the stairs to watch from my apartment window. By the time I'd reached the apartment and rushed to the window, I discovered both men had disappeared. My stomach clenched, because the trucks were still there and the men wouldn't be far from them.

I'd just leaned out the window a little further to see if I could catch a glimpse of either one of them when there was a brisk knock at my door. I jumped so high I butted my crown on the bottom edge of the window. Rubbing the knot and checking for blood, I stared at the door until another more demanding knock came.

That had to be one of them, I decided, feeling my belly clench. I really didn't feel up to a confrontation of any description, but it occurred to me that if one of them was with me, then neither of them could do anything stupid--OK, so they could, but it might avert whatever was brewing between them.

I'd already started toward the door when the banging on the panel came again. Uneasiness had been replaced by irritation as I grabbed the knob and yanked the door open. It died a quick death.

Both men were standing at my door.

I gaped at them, too stunned to think of anything at all to say. Before I could gather my wits, they'd invited themselves in. I stood holding the door knob for several moments, watching them numbly as they stalked about my living room, looking it over as if they were trying to decide where to make their mark. Footsteps in the hallway outside recalled me to the fact that I was still standing in the doorway with the door open. Glancing out at the curious neighbors, I shut the door abruptly and, feeling as if I'd just shut the lion's cage door with myself on the inside, turned to look the Beau's over uneasily.

A curious familiarity washed over me as I studied first one and then the other. I hadn't seen them side by side before, and their coloring was as nearly opposite as was possible, but oddly enough I began to notice a lot of similarity between the two. They were almost the same height and build. Not just roughly the same height and build, I mentally amended, proportionately very similar. Moreover, the shape of their faces, their lips, and even their eyes were close enough that if they hadn't had two last names, and one hadn't been dark and the other fair, I think I would've guessed them to be brothers.

I frowned. "Are you two related?" I asked before I thought better of it.

It was instantly obvious that I couldn't have found anything more calculated to rile them. They frowned at me and then turned to look each other over, their expressions eloquent of disgust--and almost identical.

"NO!"

"Not hardly!"

I pasted an uneasy smile on my lips. "Sorry! Could I get y'all something to drink?" I asked quickly, remembering my manners and realizing at the same moment that it would give me something to do to get me out of the living room.

"What've you got?"

"Sweet tea and water," I said firmly. I didn't have beer and there was no way in hell I would have offered it to them if I had. The only thing worse than having two rednecks in the house who despised each other was having two drunk rednecks in the same vicinity who hated each other.

"Tea," they both responded almost in unison, which prompted another challenging glare from both of them.

I retreated to the kitchen. My hands were shaking so badly by now that I nearly dropped the glasses I pulled from the cabinet and set on the kitchen table. I couldn't ring the damned things either, spilling nearly a glass full on the table top. Grabbing the dripping glasses, I headed back into the living room.

I almost ran into DuMauier at the door. Handing him one glass, I moved past him to head off Chevalier, who had also surged forward.

"Have a seat--Why don't you?" I said uncomfortably, wishing I could just show them both the door and indulge myself in a fit of hysteria. "I think I'll have some tea, too," I added, dashing back into the kitchen and trying to think what I was going to do about having both of them in my apartment.

I wasn't actually inclined toward claustrophobia, but these guys seemed to be sucking up all the light and air.

Neither one had actually stated their purpose, not that they needed to. It was patently obvious that the underlying motivation was to watch one another.

"I thought I'd collect on that dinner," DuMauier said from the door of the kitchen, making me jerk all over and spill the tea I'd just lifted to my lips all down the front of my blouse.

"We had a date, remember?" Chevalier growled, trying to shove his way past DuMauier, who was trying to block the door without giving the appearance that that was what he'd intended all along.

I stared at them both like a deer caught in the headlights. It took me several moments to jog my brain into gear and arrive at the realization that I hadn't actually invited either one of them. DuMauier had been a 'dinner sometime' sort of arrangement, to be determined at some future date. And Chevalier had simply invited himself back for seconds. I hadn't objected because I hadn't actually had my wits about me at the time, I wasn't really against the idea, and I was doubtful, anyway, that he'd turn up again, especially so soon.

Southern manners had been pounded into me from birth, however. Nothing short of extreme emotional upheaval could goad me into breaking the 'code'. As badly as I wanted to break free of the restraint, tell both men they were scaring the shit out of me and to get the hell out, I merely smiled weakly and tried to think up a polite excuse for why I couldn't invite them to dinner. Nothing came to me.

"Oh," I managed, trying to stall for time, trying to think of something that wouldn't take hours of preparation, because I just didn't think my nerves could take a whole evening of standing between the two of them. "I'm sure I could stir up something. Y'all are both welcome to stay ... if you like?" I ended hopefully, waiting to see if either one of them would remember their own manners and make their excuses.

They exchanged another challenging stare, each, I knew, waiting for the other to bow out. Neither did.

"Sure."

I tried to look delighted that they'd decided to stay. This was another prerequisite of the southern code of hospitality. No matter how dismayed you were, you were supposed to look delighted. "Well," I said, again sparring for wind. "Why don't y'all just make yourselves at home, watch a little TV maybe? And I'll see what I can put together."

Neither man moved.

"Shoo!" I said, waving my hands at them. "House rules--nobody in the kitchen while I'm cooking!" I said through gritted teeth, softening the order with a frozen smile.

Finally, they pushed away from the door and disappeared into the living room. I breathed a sigh of relief when I heard the TV come on, hopeful that listening to the chatter on TV might lower the tension level a little.

There wasn't a lot to choose from. I'd gotten groceries, but most of it was just for me and wouldn't begin to feed two men who worked hard for a living. I'd bought a chicken to stew for the dinner I was going to cook for DuMauier, though. Dragging it out, I looked for the biggest pot I could find, washed the chicken, and dropped it in the pot, filling it with water. Deciding I could make enough chicken and dumplings to feed a small army, I went back to the refrigerator and examined it for sides. The only thing I had in volume was salad fixings, but I decided that would work.

Once the pot began to boil, I turned the chicken to the lowest heat setting, put a lid on it and headed to my room for a shower. I didn't bother making my excuses to my 'company' for abandoning them to their own devises. I had to unwind and get out of my work clothes or I was going to drop from nervous exhaustion.

Deciding I had plenty of time to take a leisurely shower before the chicken was in any danger of scorching, I climbed in and indulged myself, poking my head out to listen every now and then for thumps that might indicate a brawl in the living room. I still hadn't decided what I was going to do by the time I got out, mostly because short of shoving them out the door I couldn't see that there was anything I could do beyond entertaining them and trying to keep the peace.

Conversation was going to be hell. I didn't know either one of them well enough to know what sort of things they were interested in. They had construction in common, but since they were rivals I certainly didn't want to direct the conversation to work. I supposed I could try to bore them away by talking about my own job, but I didn't particularly want to talk shop with two guys that would have no interest in it and doubted that would make conversation anyway. It would just be me prosing on while they listened.

So where did that leave me?

If I talked about the fish fry, that would leave DuMauier out, which would be just plain rude.

I didn't spend a lot of time worrying over my 'toilet'. By the time I got out of the bathroom, I knew the water was boiling low and I didn't have time for a long debate. Besides, primping was something one did for a date. Throwing on an oversized t-shirt and a pair of shorts, I combed my hair and hurried back to the kitchen to check the dinner.

Chevalier and DuMauier were engrossed in a forensics show as I passed through the living room, or seemed to be. Feeling more hopeful than I had since they'd arrived, I refilled the pot of stewing chicken, dropped in bullion cubes and black pepper, and then mixed up a large bowl of dumplings. The chicken still wasn't tender enough to debone by the time I'd made salads so I looked for something I could serve as 'appetisizer' to keep them occupied for a while. Again, without surprise, I saw that the pickings were slim. Unearthing a couple of small bags of chips, I dragged out a bowl and dumped them all in together, grabbed the pitcher of tea and headed into the living room to face the guests.

They'd taken up positions on either end of my couch, which wasn't a very big couch to start with. Wedging myself between them, I refilled their glasses and offered the chips. They dug in with an enthusiasm that immediately alerted me to the fact that they were hungry.

Food to soothe the savage beasts, I thought, realizing I might just come out of this relatively unscathed after all if I could keep them occupied with food. "What's happening?' I asked, pointing to the screen.

"They found a woman's torso in the swamp," Chevalier responded promptly.

"Ugh," I commented. Some pre-dinner show! "I've seen this one."

"Want to change the channel?" DuMauier offered, making me wonder if he was just eager to please or eager to find something else.

I shrugged. "I'll have to go back to the kitchen in a few minutes anyway. Y'all didn't find any sports?"

"Football season's over," they retorted at almost the same time.

Good to know, I thought. They both liked football, but had no particular interest in anything else. It was almost eerie.

Dinner went surprisingly well, all things considered. They both missed the Cajun spices absent from my efforts, but since they polished off the pot of chicken and dumplings I decided they either weren't that particular, or they thought it was good anyway.

Any hopes I'd been nursing that they would take off, or at least one would, after dinner, was dashed. We cleaned the kitchen together and filed back into the living room to watch a movie which no one was particularly interested in. Realizing fairly quickly that both of them were determined to out wait the other because they'd both decided to make a bid for spending the night, I finally reminded them that the next day was a work day and evicted them.

As happy as I was to have made it through the evening without any breakage of either their faces or my personal belongings, I was a bit miffed, too. I was wildly attracted to both men. What the hell was I going to do about it, I wondered?

Like bad pennies, they both turned up again the following night. This time I managed to make it inside and I'd just decided the experience the night before had sent them both packing when they showed up within a few minutes of each other. Both had brought dinner--Cajun style, which set me on fire since I wasn't used to spicy food, and amused both men.

I didn't want to run the gauntlet nightly, I decided. And besides, I could see I was never going to get the chance to do more than lust over them at this rate because Chevalier and DuMauier were so busy keeping each other out of my bed that I was sleeping alone.

That night, I decided to take matters into my own hands, for better or worse. Getting up the minute the evening news started, I switched the TV off and turned to confront them before they could get up and leave.

"I don't know what the history is between the two of you, but I want to make it clear right now that I don't like being in the middle of it. I like both of you. I'm not going to take sides. You are both welcome to visit any time, but unless you two are thinking about making us a threesome--because I damned sure don't want to become your buddies--then you need to come on different nights. I don't care how you settle it, as long as it isn't anywhere around me, but decide."

I saw as I let them out that I'd managed to piss both of them off. I'd reached the point where I didn't particularly care, though. I wasn't having any fun playing referee.

When neither Chevalier nor DuMauier showed up the following night, I decided I was relieved. That didn't last. I'd had more company than I knew what to do with for two nights in a row, and Chevalier the night before that. I'd hardly touched down in the city before the storm hit, and had suddenly found myself without any company at all.

It was just as well, I assured myself. They were both babe magnets. Once they'd finished squabbling over me, they would've moved on anyway, because I was fairly sure it wasn't me they wanted so much as an excuse to fight.

As if they didn't have enough excuses.

I was dying to know what the deal was between them. I didn't believe for one minute that it was just the local gene pool that had resulted in them resembling each other so strongly, any more than I believed the names were coincidental. It was possible the rivalry between them had arisen out of the battle for supremacy in the local construction industry, but I didn't believe that either. I was convinced that the rivalry went much further back and more deeply.

Unfortunately, I didn't really know anybody in town besides the Beaus, so there was no subtle way to snoop. The only way I might possibly unravel the mystery was to ask one of them point blank and after a few days with no sign of either man I'd come to the conclusion that I wasn't going to get the opportunity.

The lack of a personal life made it easy for me to throw myself into my work, and I thought by the end of the week that I'd managed to recover myself from the not-too-wonderful first day I'd had.

I was not looking forward to spending the weekend at home, alone, but I promised myself that I would use the time to explore my new home city, take in the sights--maybe meet some guy that wasn't carrying a chip on his shoulder.

With mixed feelings I discovered the rivalry had entered a new phase. Instead of the Mexican standoff, we'd entered the race, and the championship fuck-a-thon. The first guy through the door won that night's prize and did his best to prove he was the best lover.

It took me nearly a month to figure it out, though. Between the new job and the Beaus, I hardly knew which end was up. Sometimes I'd hear a knock and open the door to discover that both Beaus were standing at my door, glaring at each other. Sometimes it was DuMauier, and sometimes Chevalier. Sometimes DuMauier would be standing at my door two or three days in a row and then the next day Chevalier would show up wearing a broad grin and a black eye.

The first Friday that rolled around after the ultimatum, I answered the door and found DuMauier bearing dinner and flowers and the discolored remains of a black eye. Uneasiness immediately gripped me, but when I saw he was alone I invited him in, still nervous but so glad that I hadn't managed to run both of them off that I was willing to ignore the rough start if DuMauier seemed similarly inclined.

Trying not to think about the disappointment churning in me that my blond god had slipped through my fingers just when things had seemed so promising, I relieved DuMauier of both of his offerings and went into the kitchen with them. He was standing between me and the cabinet that held my dishes when I turned around, leaning back against the counter. His arms were crossed over his chest, his green eyes turbulent as he studied me.

I hadn't actually questioned his motives, I realized abruptly. I'd assumed I knew what they were--one upmanship on his arch rival. Now I wasn't so certain, but I was reluctant to fall for the lure of some gentler emotion, disbelieving that he'd felt any sense of betrayal or hurt over my fickleness regardless of what I saw in his eyes.

There was no rhyme or reason for him to feel any of that, and yet I couldn't shake a twinge of guilt. The flirtation we'd engaged in had been filled with promise. To my mind it had been totally sexual and I'd been convinced it was the same for him because I'd read him right away as a player. I didn't like the doubt that entered my mind as I gazed into his eyes and I didn't like the feeling creeping over me that I'd done something I shouldn't have.

Bad girl/good girl was rapidly going the way of the dinosaur and for damned good reason. It was archaic, a concept designed by men because they were territorial by nature and fostered by women who had the insane notion that they could hang on to their man if only the other women would stay away. Men were long overdue for taking responsibility for their own actions. If they made a commitment, it was their responsibility to keep it, not the women they cheated with, and unless I made a commitment, which I never had, then I was certainly under no obligation to reserve myself for one man anymore than men felt compelled to do so. Deep down, I felt--knew--that I had as much right to troll the field as anyone else, man or woman, but generations of brainwashing ran deep.

That was the source of the guilt.

That and the hint of hurt I thought I'd seen in his eyes, because I was a total pushover. I couldn't stand to think I'd hurt anyone.

But maybe my imagination was just running wild? Or maybe what I saw in his eyes was only peripherally connected to me?

I lifted my hand to his bruised cheek, brushing the pads of my fingertips over the discoloration gently. "That looks like it hurt."

He grinned, suddenly, his smile like the sun breaking over the horizon. "Mais oui, but I guarantee he looks much worse, chère."

I shook my head, realizing he'd thoroughly enjoyed the brawl, wondering abruptly if I'd been sucked in by my own weakness. "What is it with you two?" I asked with a mixture of amusement, exasperation, and genuine interest.

He uncrossed his arms, settling his hands on my upper arms and drawing me closer. "You," he murmured, his lips less than a hair's breadth from mine, his warmth, the taste of his breath on my tongue, his sheer intensity stirring currents of heat inside of me and jacking my heart rate up several notches when he hadn't even touched me yet.

"I'm not falling for that one," I whispered back, lifting my head so that my lips brushed lightly along his.

I felt as if I was falling, drowning in a sea of exquisite sensations as he opened his mouth over mine and his heat and taste and scent overwhelmed me with his first, tentative exploration of the tender flesh of my mouth. A jolt like an electric current went through me as his tongue glided coaxingly along mine, sizzling along every nerve ending and making my entire body seize. I felt an answering jolt travel through him. He lifted his head a moment to look down at me as if stunned at the magnitude of his own reaction.

Shifting his hands, he cupped my buttocks, molding me tightly against his body from waist to thigh, grinding my mound against the hard ridge that had sprung to life along the front of his jeans. Catching a handful of my hair, he tilted my head back over his arm and explored my throat thoroughly with his lips before capturing my mouth again.

This time there was no trace of uncertainty or coaxing. The urgency of his possession was demanding, rapacious and it spawned a like need in me. His hands shook slightly as they moved over me in a restless quest to touch and explore me and finally delved beneath my t-shirt, cupping each of my breasts in turn and kneading. I went directly for that hard shaft of flesh that had been bruising my mound and driving me up the wall, molding my fingers over it through his jeans and examining it from root to head.

And then examining it again with a little more disbelief than ardor because it felt like an anaconda.

There must be something in the damned water, I thought vaguely, a trace of hysterical amusement penetrating the fog of heat that had enveloped my brain, or maybe it was just the thickness of the fabric?

He bent down, dislodging my grip as he did so, nipping the painfully engorged tip of one breast. I gasped. My belly clenched at the hard current of superb sensation that speared through me. Blindly, I sought purchase and finally white knuckled the edge of the counter at the waves of dizziness and intoxicating pleasure rolling over me.

He released his prize after only a moment, straightening. Caging my face between his palms, he captured my mouth again in a deep, hungry, but disappointingly brief kiss. Catching my waist, he waltzed me in a tight turn and lifted me upwards, settling my buttocks on the countertop.

Disoriented, I clutched at his shoulders dizzily as he pushed my thighs wide and moved between them. Skimming my shirt upwards, he cupped a breast in either hand, kneading them as he suckled first one nipple and then the other, tugging at it greedily with his mouth and teasing the tip with his tongue and the edge of his teeth until I was mindless, panting, moaning. My sex quaked for him, grew wet with the need to feel him inside of me and yet I was in no particular hurry to move on. His mouth felt so good on my skin, teased me so splendidly that I wanted more, and more still.

I'd been clutching at his head, stroking his silky hair, his shoulders and back for some moments before it dawned on me that my shirt was probably suffocating him. With belated presence of mind, I tugged it off, shivering as I dropped it to the floor and reaching at once to catch hold of the back of is shirt, dragging it upward. He released me long enough to discard it, seeking my breasts again the moment he'd dropped it.

His dark olive skin was darkened from the sun, making it evident he was in the habit of discarding his shirt while he worked. His skin was smooth and silky to my touch for all that, the muscles delightfully hard beneath it.

A flicker of doubt entered my mind when I felt his tug at my waistband, but it vanished like mist as he opened the front of my jeans and delved inside with his fingers, tangling them almost painfully in the curling thatch of hair on my mound. Realizing after only a moment that the fabric and my position prevented exploration, he grabbed the waist of my jeans, peeling them off my hips. I wiggled and shifted to accommodate him, gasping as my bare ass settled on the cold countertop. He broke contact long enough to drag my jeans and panties off my legs and drew close again, pushing my thighs wider to explore my cleft with is fingers as he sought my lips once more.

I sucked in a harsh breath as he stroked the folds of skin and found my clit.

As impatient now to enter me as I was to have him inside of me, he released my lips and returned to tease my breasts. I heard the rustle of his clothes and the distinctive sound of a zipper opening, felt his movements as he pulled something from his jeans pocket.

My throat closed with need, thirst, and then my mouth watered with anticipation. I pushed away to watch while he tore open the packet. If there was a hair's worth of difference between the cock he pulled from his jeans and the one Beau Chevalier swung, I couldn't see it.

Either there was something in the water, or the two men shared the same gene pool somewhere down the line. That kind of trait had to be inherited.

He met my gaze when he'd adjusted the condom, giving me one last chance to object, I realized.

Objecting was the furthest thing from my mind. I reached for his cock, guiding it to the mouth of my sex, feeling a flood of moist, heated need as I watched his flesh penetrating mine. My heart slammed against my ribcage, began to pump frantically as I felt him stretching me. The effect was devastating to my senses. Gasping, I placed my palms on the countertop on either side of me and slightly behind me to brace myself and lifted toward him.

He wrapped an arm around my hips, taking one nipple into his mouth and sucking it hard as he thrust, embedding himself deeper by excruciating inches that left no part of my passage unscathed, untested. I felt my body quaking around his hard flesh, resisting his steady, determined thrust, held my breath until blackness crowded around me. Sucking in a harsh breath as he withdrew slightly and pushed again, I lifted my legs, locking my ankles around his waist and using my thighs to draw him toward me.

We were both panting for breath, gasping as if we were dying, moist with sweat by the time he'd embedded his flesh completely inside of me and began to move, slowly at first, but rapidly increasing the tempo as the delicious friction of our bodies broke what little control remained to us.

Trembling, weak, dizzy, I looped an arm around his neck, nuzzling my face against his neck and nibbling at the flesh, sucking love bites as I felt myself tightening toward explosion, sucking harder as my body suddenly erupted in sharp convulsions of unadulterated pleasure. He groaned as my passage quaked around his flesh, clenched and unclenched with the spasms that rocked me, began to milk him. He dragged in a shaky breath, faltered and then began to pump into me faster and harder. The tremors traveling through him became hard quakes. He stilled save for the uncontrollable shudders, gasping hoarsely for a moment and then seeking my lips, kissing my lips ravenously as his body culminated and finally breaking to kiss my neck as his body began to drift toward calm.

Thoroughly spent, we leaned together weakly, nuzzling each other gratefully. It was some moments before I realized he was murmuring to me in French. My mind was so much mush, my pounding heart and rasping breath deafening me until I'd thought at first I just couldn't make out the words. I hadn't a clue of what he was murmuring. Shit sounded beautiful in French as far as I was concerned. He might have been telling me I was a delightfully nasty bitch. I didn't care. I loved the sound of it and his body language was telling me it was something I would've liked if I could've kicked my brain into gear enough to translate.

It occurred to me after a moment, though, that what he was saying probably wouldn't be anything I'd learned in French class.

I struggled for a few moments to think of some kind of response and finally just settled for a bit more nuzzling and stroking. His body was a pure delight to touch and fondle.

He drew away slightly after a moment, caught my cheeks between his palms and studied my face. A faint smile curled his lips. "I should feed you before I breed you, eh, petit?"

I chuckled. "I forgot about the food," I said wryly.

"Me, as well, but I'll not complain about what you're serving in this kitchen, chère," he murmured, fitting his lips to mine briefly and then carefully pulling his flesh from mine and retreating in the direction of the bathroom.

Sighing, I scooted off the counter. After a moment's consideration, I left the jeans where they lay and merely pulled on the t-shirt. Taking one plate down, I heated up an assortment of the food he'd brought. I'd just set the plate on the table with two glasses of tea when he returned. He ran a palm down my bare ass, lifting his dark brows at me questioningly. Giving him a provocative smile, I pushed him toward the chair I'd positioned beside the table and straddled his lap once he'd sat down, looping one arm around his neck.

His eyes glittered with a mixture of desire and interest as I fed him a bite of food with my fingers and then sucked the residue from the tips. He shifted uncomfortably as he watched my fingers disappear into my mouth. He took another bite and grimaced, looking distinctly uncomfortable. "This will end badly, chère," he murmured with a trace of amusement and a good deal of disappointment. "One raincoat I carry in case it rains. But I had not anticipated it would, and certainement had not expected a flood."

I couldn't help but chuckle at his quaint way of putting it, or be pleased that he hadn't expected me to be a pushover, but I couldn't deny that I was also very disappointed to discover I wasn't getting desert. The main course had been delicious. I was sated, but it had only wetted my appetite for more.

I searched my mind for a solution, but realized even before I tried that I was going to come up empty. I hadn't had a supply of condoms on hand since I'd broken off with my last significant other over a year before because I'd just been too busy with work to even consider looking around for a replacement.

"You have any raincoats at your place?" I asked tentatively as I fed myself a bite of fish and then allowed him to suck the rest off of my fingers, enjoying the heat stirring in my belly as he sucked the digits one by one.

He frowned pensively at the question. After a moment his skin darkened and he shook his head. "There as been a drought of late," he responded with a self depreciating grin.

I gave him a look of patent disbelief. I hadn't seen any females hanging after him at his place, true, but I'd assumed that was because he preferred to keep his stable off premises to keep from running the risk of being caught between two indignant females. "How long a drought?" I asked after a moment, leaning toward him and nipping at his hard jaw with my teeth.

He said nothing. When I leaned back to study his face, I saw that his expression was closed. His gaze flickered away from mine. He swallowed thickly. "I should go, I think," he muttered.

I tightened my arms around his neck, more from an instinctive need to know what was bothering him than design. "What is it?"

He caught my hips in his hands, tightened them as if he would lift me away from him. "Six months? Perhaps a year? Guilt does nothing for the ardor," he muttered, setting me from his lap gently, but resolutely, and rising abruptly. "We argued. She left in tears and wrapped the car around a bridge piling."

"Oh my god," I gasped, too shocked to fully take it in. "Your girl friend?"

"My wife."

* * * *

I'm pretty sure I'd never felt more like a horse's ass than I did as I stood like I'd been pole axed and watched Beau DuMauier's departure. I don't know what made me feel worse, the fact that I'd completely misjudged the guy, or the fact that I'd so been so completely insensitive and superficial.

The fact was, I put on a good show, but I wasn't insensitive at all. I was no stranger to tragedy myself, and I was empathetic to a painful degree, which was why I'd learned to hold life at arm's length.

I don't know who the idiot was that thought up the sentiment 'better to have loved and lost than never to have loved at all' but I was convinced he was either a masochist or completely unable to feel anything deeply at all because it took more guts than I had to open myself wide for another dose of misery.

Not that I'd ever actually been in love. I'd had a crush on a guy in high school, which had taught me why they called it a crush, because I had been certain I loved him desperately and when he dumped me for another girl a steamroller couldn't have flattened me any more effectively.

It was hard to say which was worse, losing someone you loved to life or losing someone you loved to death. Either way it was forever and time only dulled the pain. I knew it never completely went away as long as one still drew breath.

I didn't doubt for a moment that what he'd told me was the truth. I'd seen it in his eyes the moment I met him. I just hadn't wanted to see it and I'd ignored it.

I was torn. Part of me desperately wanted to comfort him, because that was just the sort of idiot I was, a total glutton for punishment. The coward in me wanted to flee, and the sex crazed part of me wanted to fuck him blind and drown his sorrows in an orgy of the senses that left no room for worries, doubts, or thought.

The wounded, I knew, though, were too vulnerable for games of any kind. Uncomplicated sex might help him, and it might not. If I'd thought it would, and I'd thought I could still hold him at arm's length emotionally speaking, I would've been more than willing to give it a try, but I seriously doubted he'd be back.

I was fiercely glad I'd behaved like a slut, because now he wouldn't be nearly as vulnerable, me being a 'bad' girl, and I wouldn't succumb to somebody that was needy, but didn't especially want or need me to fill the vacuum.

It was a close call, but due to my single minded determination to remain aloof from the rest of the world, I'd escaped relatively unscathed.

I tried to soothe my discomfort by telling myself that I'd been good for him. Obviously, he'd needed to get laid, and the brawl that he'd had with the other Beau had probably helped him let off a lot of pent up frustration and pain.

If it wasn't just like me to screw everything up. Two absolutely divine hunks and I'd blown it with both of them! I could fuck up a wet dream!

Two days later I discovered I was wrong on both counts because I opened my door and discovered both Beaus trying to stare each other down. I was so relieved that I was going to get another chance, I beamed at both of them. "Hi! Y'all come in!"

Chevalier stepped inside. DuMauier remained where he was. "I just came by to ask you out to dinner."

"Actually, that was what I had in mind," Chevalier growled, "and I was here first."

I grabbed DuMauier's hand and dragged him inside. "I'll cook. It's a work night and I don't like going out during the week."

The two men exchanged a look, obviously debating with themselves whether or not they wanted to leave the field wide open for the other one. Leaving them to make up their minds whether to go or stay, I flipped the TV on and headed into the kitchen.

"I just happen to have a couple of steaks," I called enticingly.

DuMauier appeared at the kitchen door. "I could grill them."

I smiled at him. "Great! We can all go to your place."

He sent me a narrow eyed glare but after a moment turned and looked a question at Chevalier.

"Why the fuck not?" Chevalier growled, getting to his feet and stomping out the door. "I'll go grab some beer."

A stab of uneasiness went through me but I figured if the brew got fireworks started I could always decamp, head for my place, and call the cavalry before things got completely out of hand.

The guys never failed to surprise me. If I'd been a betting woman, I'd have bet when Chevalier peeled out of the apartment complex that he was gone for good, if not for the night. He came back with a case of beer just as DuMauier threw the steaks on the grill. If I'd been stupid, and egotistical, I might have preened myself over it, but I didn't suffer from either problem.

These two loved tormenting each other better than anybody I knew.

And it occurred to me that the beer might just loosen their tongues and satisfy my curiosity. I took one, more to be companionable than because I had any interest in it. Piss probably tasted better. While Chevalier paced DuMauier's patio like a caged lion, I went back to my place to cook up some potatoes to go with them and mix up a salad. By the time I got back, Chevalier had mellowed and sprawled in a handy lawn chair. DuMauier was looking a bit more mellow, too.

They were talking shop when I arrived. Smiling inwardly, I asked for directions to DuMauier's kitchen and took the food inside. It was immediately apparent when I stepped in the door that, contrary to popular belief, not all men lived like pigs when they had no woman around. DuMauier's place didn't look like the pad of a neat freak, but it was well kept.

There were marks on the wall in the hallway where pictures had once hung.

I tried not to think about that. Resisting the urge to snoop, I found the bathroom. I met up with DuMauier on the way out. "I hope you don't mind?" I asked belatedly.

He shook his head. "The steaks are ready if you like rare."

I wrinkled my nose. "Medium, please."

Nodding, he grabbed a platter from the kitchen.

"I'll set the table," I offered, having followed him.

He hooked an arm around my waist as I came even with him, dragging me up against him. I looked up at him in surprise and met him in descent. His kiss was hot, possessive and laden with promise that made me tingle all the way down to my toes. His eyes were tumultuous when he lifted his head. "You are playin' with fire, petit," he growled. "You know this?"

I shivered when he released me, but I realized I was a moron after all. I was way more thrilled than unnerved.

When he'd gone, I looked at my half finished beer suspiciously, and finally poured the rest down the sink and tossed the bottle in the recycle bin.

I was playing with fire. I knew I was, but, damn it! I wanted both of them. I really, really liked both. Why should I have to choose, especially when they were making it so that I didn't have to?

I didn't care if I was being unreasonable about it. It wasn't as if either one of them was being exactly reasonable and, besides, I was in serious trouble. I knew that without both to act as buffers for each other I was going to fall like a ton of bricks for one of them.

If I'd had the acute sense of self preservation I'd thought I had I would've refused to see either one of them.

By the time I'd set plates out and gotten the salad out of the refrigerator, DuMauier had returned bearing the platter full of steaks. Chevalier was right behind him carrying three bottles of beer.

I settled in the seat between the two of them and studied the beer Chevalier set beside my plate. The kiss, and/or the warning DuMauier had given me had pierced my buzz and I decided as I surveyed the brooding glitter in both men's eyes that I'd just have another.

The second beer tasted somewhat better than the first--which was to say I managed to swallow without gagging. "The steak is fabulous," I announced once I'd had my first bite and put out the fire from the spices he'd used to season the meat with another sip. "You're right, Beau, you do cook a mean steak."

He exchanged a glance with Chevalier and a smile dawned. "How many of those have you had, chère?"

I looked at him in surprise. "Those what?"

"The beer," Chevalier supplied, the look in his eyes making me hot all over.

"Oh! Only half," I said airily. "I don't much care for it to be perfectly honest with you, but it's good with the steak," I added politely to Chevalier since he was the one who'd brought it.

We'd been eating in silence for several minutes when I suddenly recalled that I'd figured the guys would be more talkative once they had a few beers. "Ok," I said conversationally, "so I'm figuring I'm probably the only person in the state that hasn't got a fucking clue of what the deal is between you two."

They both stopped eating, exchanged a challenging glare and then, after glancing at me, went back to their steaks.

"Is there some reason why I shouldn't know?" I tried again.

Chevalier finally sat back in his seat, eyeing me for several moments. "Once upon a time, our mothers were best friends."

I blinked several times, wondering what I'd missed. Obviously, that comment was supposed to make everything crystal clear to me. I gave the nearly empty bottle of beer a distrustful look. "But they're not any more?" I guessed finally, wondering what the hell that had to do with the Beaus.

"No," DuMauier said coolly, eyeing Chevalier now with patent hostility.

I was having a hard time grasping the undertones here. Why would DuMauier and Chevalier be so hostile toward each other when the dispute was between their mothers? I didn't give a shit who my mother fought with as long as I was a good mile or two down the road before the fireworks started. Sometimes I even actually agreed with her, but I couldn't recall ever feeling this militant about something that really wasn't any of my business.

That teased my drunken brain for several moments and it finally dawned on me that the only reason why they would take it personally was because it was personal.

Best friends--and both men had the same name.

"You're not going to tell me this is about one of your mother's stealing the other one's baby name?" I asked, suddenly enlightened because I remembered my sister and her sister-in-law had just about had a knock down drag out cat fight about the names they'd picked out when both of them were expecting at almost the same time.

Chevalier gave me an even look. "It was my father's name," he said grimly.

I stared at him blankly. I was within a hair's breadth of saying 'so?' when lightening struck me. "Oh!" I said, realizing it wasn't just the name. "Oh!" I said again, glancing from one to the other and remembering I'd wondered, out loud, if they were related. Chevalier's mother, I realized suddenly, suspected her best friend was sleeping with her husband and the woman had had the balls to name her son after the father!

I hopped up from the table in a blind panic. "Jesus fucking Christ! What time is it? I have to go now. I really enjoyed the dinner and the company guys, but I have to work tomorrow and I just remembered I haven't done the laundry!"

* * * *

I honestly didn't want to get caught in the middle of the Beau's blood feud. I wouldn't have become involved with either one of them, at all, if I'd had any inkling of what I was getting myself into. But then I had been pretty thoroughly snagged even before I'd tumbled to the fact that my gorgeous neighbor and the equally divine blond god I'd met by chance weren't just coincidentally both babe magnets. Obviously, it was a family trait, because they had charisma that went well beyond their physical desirability.

Unfortunately, I was in deep before I'd realized that this was not something I could skim through, enjoy myself thoroughly, and then just go on my merry way. It was worse that I also realized that I was probably the only one in this menage a` trois that was emotionally involved and sinking fast. I adored both of them. What had started as a single minded pursuit of pleasure had evolved beyond that because I'd gotten caught up in their painful drama.

I thought Beau DuMauier was the most needy of the two and probably more like me than I liked to think. It seemed to me that the world had been trying to crush him from birth. I blamed his mother for most of that. Of course, I had no idea what the circumstances were. She might have been just as helplessly entangled in that web as I was in mine. I wasn't sure at this point if I even wanted to know what those circumstances were, but however she'd gotten caught up in the triangle, it seemed to me that her son had caught hell for it, maybe more than she had and maybe not, but more than he'd deserved certainly.

He'd been deprived of both a father and a brother. No one had allowed him to forget that he was a bastard growing up in a time when it was still a heavy stigma, but he'd beat the odds. He'd made something of himself despite everything.

And then there was the latest blow.

The wound seemed pretty raw, but from what he had told me, I decided DuMauier must have lost his wife the year before. He'd said guilt didn't do anything for his ardor and, before he taken the plunge with me, he hadn't been with anybody for six months to a year. Given his grief, I didn't make the mistake of thinking that reference had anything to do with his late wife. I was completely certain he knew exactly when his wife had died--but he might or might not clearly remember his attempts to 'pick up' life afterwards.

It was sufficient that it seemed like a very long time to him.

I took heart in it anyway, hoping it must mean that I wasn't going to discover I was his rebound.

I thought in a way he probably needed the feud. As tumultuous as it made his life, it gave him an outlet for his pain that he probably needed, and I thought he also preferred fighting with his brother than simply being ignored because it gave him a link that he wouldn't have had otherwise.

That thought brought me to the relationship I'd seen between Chevalier and his 'real brothers', the ones he claimed. I wondered if DuMauier was aware of that close click that he was excluded from and decided he probably was. It was a big city, but he was still close enough to the family he'd probably watched from the outside his entire life.

Chevalier seemed a happy go lucky sort, or he had when I'd met him and I had to admit he seemed to have every reason to be. He hailed from a large very close knit family and although they were by no means wealthy as far as I could see his background had given him a healthy emotional stability to be a success.

Regardless, I knew there had to be some deep wound he kept hidden. I knew he adored his mother. That closeness had been easy to see when I'd joined the family gathering. But I didn't think that really accounted for his ongoing feud with his half brother. I was pretty sure he kept it going because he was as determined to have some link with his unacceptable sibling regardless of the unfortunate situation as DuMauier was.

My conclusion from all that was not a happy one. They were using me to get at each other.

Ordinarily, that wouldn't have bothered me. I didn't want to get emotionally entangled anyway and the situation should have been perfect--a balance between having fun and company without any strings attached. In this case, though, I was already regretting that there weren't going to be any strings. The more time I spent with them the more certain I was that I was the only one that was going to get hurt here. I was going to get hooked on them and then they were going to move on to another battle ground.

God only knew how many they'd already fought over--the fact that they'd both named their construction companies after their father was certainly one, and one that guaranteed a running battle as long as they kept the companies going.

The question was, what was I going to do about the situation? Simply going with the flow wasn't going to work for me this time.

Maybe, I decided, what I needed to do was to think about somebody else for a change? I did adore them both and I did thoroughly enjoy this duel they had going to prove themselves with me by fucking me silly, but it was going to end unhappily for me whatever I tried to do. Maybe it was time I took one of those knocks I was always running from and tried to make things come out better for someone else even if I did get hurt?

After a bit more thought it dawned on me that, just maybe, I'd already fallen into the way of things by not retreating the moment I discovered the situation I'd gotten myself into. The Beaus had probably spent more time in the same vicinity since I'd arrived than they had in their entire lives before. The hostility was palpable most of the time, of course, but they'd actually spoken fairly civilly to each other on a few occasions.

That was bad news for me, of course. They both knew they were sleeping with me. If they could be civil at all it meant that I wasn't that important to them, but as unhappy as that made me I couldn't very well complain. It was my own fault for not ditching one of them right off.

I decided I wasn't going to regret that. I was going to go on enjoying the situation as long as I could and, maybe, after it was all over and done with they would at least remember me fondly.

I would just let things go on as they had been. Both of them were stubborn, but they were getting used to being around each other. Maybe if I just dropped a subtle hint now and then I could make them both come around to thinking that there was no sense at all in them continuing to punish each other for their parent's mistakes.

The next time they both showed up at my door together, I invited them in as always and braced myself for an explosive confrontation. It took a lot of bracing for me. Ordinarily I tucked my tail and headed for the hills if there was even an indication there might be one.

I was armed, though. I'd gotten the fixings for chicken and dumplings again, because I could tell they'd really enjoyed them, and I'd gotten a six pack of beer--just enough to help them to mellow a bit and, hopefully, not enough to get them to the point of belligerence.

After dinner, when we settled on the couch to squabble over what to watch, I handed the 'scepter' over to Chevalier and looked DuMauier over speculatively. "I met Chevalier's family and they're a real trip. I haven't met any of your family, though," I said, trying to sound like it was merely friendly interest. "Don't they live around here?"

He met my gaze, but his expression was closed and he merely grunted. "No."

"He doesn't have any family," Chevalier volunteered.

I glanced at Chevalier in surprise. I didn't have to feign it because I was surprised that he seemed to know that much about DuMauier. When I turned to look at DuMauier again, I saw that he seemed as surprised as I was.

"I can't imagine what that would be like," I said with sympathy and with complete sincerity. "I think I fight with my family more than we get along, especially my older sister, but it's good to know they're there, because even when I'm alone, which I am a lot of the time, I don't really feel like I'm alone. I know all I have to do is pick up the phone and I can talk to somebody that I could tell anything to."

DuMauier shrugged. "You doan miss what you never had."

I frowned. "I think I do. I always wished I'd had brothers. Not that I wanted to trade my sisters for a brother, but my mother and father divorced when I was pretty young and I just felt like I'd missed something by not having a brother around."

I glanced at Chevalier and decided not to push my luck. He was intelligent. He didn't need for me to drive it in with a sledge hammer, I didn't think. Surely he had to be considering how close he was to the brothers he claimed.

* * * *

I don't know how I managed to make it to the door unless it was familiarity with the apartment because I still hadn't managed to get my eyes open more than a crack when I opened the door. DuMauier looked at me uncomfortably. "I woke you, chère?"

My brain wasn't really functioning either. "No!" I replied automatically. "What day is it?"

A slow grin curled his lips. "I should come back later."

I wanted to go back to bed, badly, but not necessarily alone. I grabbed his wrist and urged him inside. "Come snuggle me," I said with a yawn, "and we'll discuss it when I wake up."

I left him to lock the door--or not, and staggered back toward the bedroom. Crashing into the mattress, I lost consciousness again immediately. I woke sometime later to find a mouth attached to one nipple. Unwilling to give up on sleep altogether, I tried to ignore it for a while, but the insistent tugging generated heat at my core that smoldered and finally caught fire. Groaning, I threaded my fingers through the silky hair on the head attached to that delicious mouth.

As if he'd only been waiting for that reaction, he let go of it and caught hold of the nipple on the other peak. Since it had been ignored up to that point, and was throbbing like an aching tooth, the first hard drag on it from that hot mouth sent electrifying currents through me. I was just starting to really enjoy it when he stopped.

Feeling cool air waft over me, I lifted one eyelid high enough to see if he was abandoning me or changing positions.

He was naked and beautiful to behold in the morning light filtering into the room. I opened the other eye to fully appreciate the lovely view as he knelt over my legs and caught hold of my panties, dragging them down my legs. As I pulled my feet from the panties, I bent my knees and set my soles flat on the bed, spreading my thighs wide.

He moved between my legs pushing my thighs wider as he leaned over me.

It wasn't much by way of foreplay, but I wasn't going to complain. I was ready. My kegels had been clapping together and shouting 'come and get it' from the moment he'd grabbed hold of nipple number two and set fire to my blood.

He was ready too, his cock rock hard, the flesh so engorged his skin was glossy.

He wasn't wearing a condom, and I lifted my gaze to his questioningly. His green eyes were smoldering with desire and intent, his face harsh with it. My heart executed a strange little flutter as it dawned on me what he was doing, what he was saying.

He settled over me, supporting himself on one arm as he guided his cock into my passage and thrust upward. When he'd firmly embedded the head into my passage, he planted that arm on the other side of me and slipped it beneath my shoulders.

Supporting himself on his elbows, hovering mere inches above me, he watched my face as he pressed deeper, eased off, and then pressed again, sheathing his flesh by patient inches within my channel in a way that pushed what little patience I had right out of my mind. I was panting for breath by the time he had buried himself to the hilt inside of me. He was shaking, his skin moist, but he went still for many moments, merely lying on top of me, his flesh joined with mine.

It was like nothing I'd ever experienced in my life, completely sexual, and yet more.

My throat tightened as if an invisible hand was strangling me as I stared deeply into his eyes.

I don't know if he saw what he was looking for in my eyes or not, but he seemed to, because after a moment, he closed the distance that separated us and covered my mouth in a heated kiss that made the smoldering flames inside of me leap upward into a conflagration. Unable to hold still any longer, I arched against him.

Either his control broke, or I broke it. I wasn't certain which, and I didn't care. I didn't need a slow build up. I needed forceful, masterful penetration. He gave it to me, holding me tightly to keep from driving me up the bed, stroking my g-spot with enough friction to light my fire. I ran for it, reached the summit and leapt off into glory, closing my eyes as my body performed the 9th Opus, complete with symbols and fireworks.

I figured it was as close to heaven as I was ever likely to get.

It almost seemed symbolic, somehow, that we came together--like the joining thing--the trust he'd shown me. Because he wasn't careless. He wasn't one of those men that just didn't want anything to come between him and his pleasure. He considered having sex with me, having safe sex.

I felt like crying for no reason that I could think of.

Because I was moved?

I was, but I wasn't sure that was all of it.

I was distressed, because he cared--and I cared, and even so I couldn't put the other Beau out of my mind.

It wasn't supposed to get this complicated.

There was tenderness in his touch and in the kisses he lavished on me in the aftermath. That was the crowning touch, making it absolutely impossible for me to pretend it was just another good fuck.

Damn it!

I tried to put a good face on it, doing my utmost to pretend in spite of hell that we'd just had a grand, impersonal roll that had been mutually satisfying, knowing if he gave me that hurt look I saw in his eyes sometimes I was just going to squall like a baby.

"Awake now, chère?" he asked after a few moments, drawing away.

I blinked, but I was heartened by the cheerfulness in his voice. "Don't tell me! You want seconds?"

He chuckled huskily. "I thought you might like to take a ride with me."

My mind instantly began to computate a list of the things I needed to do over the weekend. "Sure!"

He chuckled as I slipped out of the bed and headed toward the shower. "You doan wanna ask where, chère? How long we'll be gone?"

I threw a smiling glance at him. "Nope. I'll be with you. That's all that matters."

I cringed once I'd stepped out of view. Stupid! Distance girl, I chided myself! The last thing I wanted to do was to precipitate a 'moment', one of those moments of truth where one of the party decided to take a leap the other party wasn't ready for and it ended up ruining everything for both of them.

I'd known the moment would come long ago, weeks, almost from the very first, in fact. I was actually surprised that both Beaus were still hanging around me, because I'd absolutely refused, regardless of the enticement, to be the one to make the decision. I adored both of them--really, really liked them. More than liked them, truth be told. I didn't want to choose and I wasn't going to let them make me. I'd continued to see both of them, with their full knowledge.

Well, I'd sort of expected it. More accurately, I'd thought the moment of truth, if there was one, was going to be a demand from either DuMauier or Chevalier to choose, and when I couldn't, they'd both be out the door.

They surprised me, because neither one demanded it. They competed, and it was clear they were trying to prove to me which was the better man, but they'd never come right out and laid down the law. When they'd begun to get along, I'd thought that was it--not that they always got along, but I hadn't noticed any indication of a fist fight in weeks, and on those occasions when they both showed up at my place, they were often downright cordial.

DuMauier surprised me by heading out of the city. He smiled faintly when I glanced at him, knowing I was curious. I studied his profile, trying to decide whether he wanted me to play a guessing game or if he wanted to surprise me with whatever 'treat' he had in mind.

I wondered if it had anything to do with the 'for sale' sign he'd put up on his front lawn the week before. I hadn't asked him about that, though.

It wasn't my business and I figured if it meant he was moving away, I just didn't want to face it until I had to.

He hadn't said anything about moving in with me.

I told myself I was glad he was selling the place, for his sake. It was hard enough to deal with grief without constant reminders and the house he'd built for the wife that died had to be hell to live in alone.

I'd never felt comfortable going there. Either he'd realized that, or he just wasn't comfortable having his fuck buddy in his wife's house. By mutual consent, we'd always met on my territory.

I preferred it that way.

We didn't go far after we'd left the city limits before DuMauier turned off onto a narrow, two lane highway. About fifteen minutes later, he slowed as he reached a fancy stone work entranceway and turned off of that onto a newly paved road.

Up and down the road, I saw houses that looked like young mansions--not the sort of mansions the filthy rich built for themselves, but still two or three times the size of a budget home. Awed, I stared at the houses in varying stages of completion as DuMauier slowed the truck to allow me to gawk. "They're beautiful!" I breathed, totally impressed. "You're going to be building some of these?"

He grinned.

Rounding a curve in the road, he pulled the truck off in front of a wooded lot that had just been cleared. Too impatient to wait for him to come around to open my door, I opened it myself and leapt out. He met me at the front of the truck, giving me a disapproving look. "Don't give me that sour puss look of yours," I chided him, grabbing two handfuls of flesh along his sides and tickling him.

I'd found out entirely by accident that he was ticklish, and due to my difficult nature I couldn't resist any opportunity to tease him.

He hated it when I tickled him.

Grunting, he grabbed my hands, and jerked me against his chest.

I beamed up at him, pleased that I'd managed to get a rise out of him. Usually, he tried to pretend it didn't bother him.

He gazed back at me with a mixture of irritation and amusement. But that look was back, too, the one that made me squirm inside.

Terrified that he was going to put me on the spot by saying something, I nipped at his chin and demanded to be shown the mansion he was building. He kissed me, briefly, and pulled away, catching my hand and drawing me toward the curb.

A big sign had been set into the dirt near the edge of the road. I glanced at it happily, read 'Beauregard Construction' on it and threw him a pleased look. I'd already walked past it when something about the sign struck me as odd. Halting abruptly, I retraced my steps and looked at the sign again.

Beneath the bold lettering that said 'Beauregard Construction' were two names in smaller print---Beauregard Chevalier and Beauregard DuMauier, Owners.

DuMauier was studying my face when I looked up at him, completely floored.

"You're ... y'all are building this together?"

He smiled wryly. "Partners. This way we figured we could pool our resources and get bigger jobs. We've got firm commitments on nearly half the houses planned for this subdivision."

Uttering a whoop of pure delight, I threw myself at him and hugged him. "I am so happy for you two! This is fantastic! You guys are going to be so rich! I know you will! You're both just the best carpenters, and so smart and good at everything! You'll make an unbeatable team!"

He chuckled as I pulled away from him. "How do you know we are great carpenters, chère? You have not once seen the houses we build."

I shrugged. "I don't need to. Y'all get more work than the rest. That's proof enough that you're good. Besides, I know you two! Y'all are great at everything."

Something flickered in his eyes at that and, realizing I'd probably just stuck my foot in my mouth, I grabbed his arm and urged him to show me the house.

There wasn't actually a house to see, yet. The batter boards were up, though, and the footprint had been marked. He walked me around the site, pointing out where the garage would be and the vestibule. I stared at the bare dirt a while, trying to imagine what the place would look like and finally allowed him to drag me away to show me the lot itself. The lot was huge, and had some beautiful trees on it, which they'd carefully tagged to keep the guy with the bulldozer clear of them.

When we reached the truck again, he flipped the back of the seat forward and pulled a roll of blueprints out to show me the architect's rendering of the house and the floor plan. "God! It's a monster! And so complicated," I said a little doubtfully. "Or does it just seem that way to me because I can't read blue prints?"

He shrugged. "It's no simple structure. The ceilings here and here will require master carpenters. The roof system, as well."

I studied him as he rolled the plans up carefully and secured them with a rubber band. Few carpenters ever managed to afford the homes they built. I'd always thought that was a sad thing, that they spent their lives building such beautiful homes for other people when it was something they couldn't even hope to have.

"You'll have something like this one day," I said.

He nodded. "In fact, this one."

I glanced at him sharply. "You're serious?"

He shrugged. "It's a spec house Chevalier and I are building. We decided we would live here ourselves for a while, maybe, and then sell later if we decided to part ways, or if we just needed to. In the meantime, we're hoping it'll make the company look very good."

"Oh ... my ... god!" I exclaimed, uncertain of whether I was more awed by the fact that they'd partnered to build the house, or that they'd decided to live in the grand thing.

But image, I reminded myself, could be everything. Success bred success and if they lived in a place like this it would almost certainly make them that much more desirable as contractors.

The payments would be easier with both of them chipping in, too. This wasn't the sort of house people on average incomes could afford. It took two people with very good salaries to pay for them--or one person with a huge salary.

"I guess that's why you put your house on the market?"

Again, he shrugged, but he was frowning now. "Partly. I don't need two houses, and two mortgage payments."

I didn't press it. He was still struggling, but he was trying to let go of the guilt and grief, and selling the house would be a good place to start.

* * * *

I was flattered and extremely pleased when Chevalier invited my to his apartment the next night and I arrived to discover DuMauier was there, as well. We went together, the three of us, to celebrate their new partnership.

We drank toasts to everything and had to take a cab back to Chevalier's apartment. The three of us were feeling pretty amorous by the time we'd negotiated the stairs to Chevalier's apartment and managed to get the door open.

I was anyway. Deciding to dispense with formalities, I kissed both of them, one at the time, of course, and told them they were my most favorite, favorite people in the whole wide world and I loved them both. And then I bid them a good night, stripped and crawled into the middle of Chevalier's bed.

I was completely aware it wasn't my bed, or my apartment, but I was in no condition to find my apartment, and I wasn't going home without getting laid if I could help it. I figured first man to follow was going to get lucky, and I'd catch up with the other one later.

DuMauier and Chevalier gave each other a baleful glare, but Chevalier finally dragged a coin out of his pocket. "Heads or tails?"

"Nobody's getting tails!" I informed them. "Those things are too big to be trying to stick them up my ass!"

DuMauier chuckled. Chevalier sent me a cocky grin.

Chevalier won the toss, but I figured I was the real winner, because I got DuMauier for desert.

It was a hell of a job keeping two such divine hunks satisfied, but somebody had to do it!

* * * *

It took forever to finish the house, mostly because we fought all the way through the process. I was invited to become partner number three because neither of the Beaus felt comfortable with interior design and they depended upon me to make sure they were comfortable.

It wasn't marriage, 2.5 kids and a white picket fence. It was a corporation, two kids, and a five and half thousand square foot house with a whirlpool tub, but I'd never been a traditional girl and I was perfectly satisfied with the way things turned out.

Beau Chevalier's mother didn't approve of our strange relationship at all, but when I presented her with a grandson the year after I produced DuMauier's bouncing baby girl, she decided to unbend sufficiently to acknowledge my existence.

My mother didn't approve for that matter.

But I figured she was just jealous!

The End

Printed in the United States
61567LVS00001B/163-174